NINE LIVES, ZERO PAPERWORK

9 LIVES, ∞ LIES

KYSA STEELE

Nine Lives, Zero Paperwork

Nine Lives, Infinite Lies: Book 1

1st edition: 2025
ISBN: 978-1-971434-00-1 Paperback
ISBN: 978-1-971434-01-8 Hardback
ISBN: 978-1-971434-11-7 Mass Market Paperback

To Brentley and Ashleigh—
You know who you are. I love you both.
The taco cat story is coming. Eventually.

CONTENTS

CHAPTER 1

THE IMPACT

The coffee tasted like burnt plastic.

Jarik stared into his mug—chipped ceramic that had survived three crash landings and one divorce—and wondered, not for the first time, why he'd chosen this life. The brown liquid inside had a film on top. It wasn't supposed to have a film. The *Marginal Profit* was all he had left though. Six years of his life poured into a ship that was slowly dying underneath him.

"Status report Val," he muttered.

Val responded with a crackling wheeze. "All systems functional. The left stabilizer is vibrating at the wrong frequency again. Cargo bay door is stuck half-open."

"Can you close it?"

"It thinks it's already closed."

"That doesn't make sense."

"Take it up with the door."

Jarik rubbed his temples. The *Marginal Profit* limped through the Glitter Belt Nebula at half speed. Outside the viewport, space glittered with crystallized stardust—beautiful, but hell on the sensors.

"Shortcut," he muttered. "Save three days, they said. Avoid the Interstellar Transit Authority checkpoints, they said."

Val crackled. "I did warn you."

"You said 'this route has a fifteen percent chance of catastrophic malfunction.'"

"Exactly. Warning."

Jarik was about to point out that fifteen percent wasn't exactly reassuring when the proximity alarm went off. Not the polite chirp of passing traffic—the full panic-inducing klaxon for imminent collision.

THWUMP.

The impact threw Jarik forward. The mug slipped from his three-fingered grip, spilling coffee across the console. A panel sparked—fine three seconds ago, now spitting fire. The lights cycled red, yellow, then settled on a purple that had no business being there.

Of course. The thought arrived flat and cold. *A shortcut to save three days ends with a hull breach. Perfect.*

The coffee machine ground and rattled in the galley. It had been doing that for weeks.

"What—" Jarik lunged for the controls, "—was THAT?"

"We hit something."

"Hit something? We're in SPACE!"

"Yes. I'm recalculating the statistical likelihood of—"

"Just show me the cameras!"

Jarik pulled up the external feeds, cycling through views. Cargo bay: still attached. Hull plating: intact. Port side: nothing. Starboard: nothing. Forward view—

He stopped. His mouth fell open.

There pressed against the viewport like someone's idea of a practical joke was a cat.

An actual cat. Orange tabby. Plastered against the hull in

hard vacuum, staring directly into the camera with enormous amber eyes.

Jarik blinked. The cat remained.

"Val?"

"Yes?"

"There's a cat on my windshield."

"Confirmed. There is a biological entity matching the classification 'domestic feline' on the forward viewport." Val's tone shifted, processing. "Sub-classification detected: Familiar. Mythological designation. Statistical probability of encounter: 0.00003 percent. Disregarding as sensor error."

"It's not an error. I'm looking right at it!"

"Then I have no explanation for its continued existence in hard vacuum."

"How is it alive?"

"Unknown. It's not wearing a space suit."

"I can SEE that!"

The cat ignored the vacuum. The cold. The several thousand kilometers per hour. Fur rippling in a breeze that shouldn't exist. Tail swishing.

Its mouth moved. Jarik leaned forward. Squinted. The cat's lips formed deliberate shapes—intentional communication. The words were obvious:

You missed the turnoff.

"That's impossible," Jarik said.

"Which part?"

"All of it!"

The cat raised one paw. Tapped the windshield. Three precise taps. *Tink. Tink. Tink.* The sound echoed through the cabin—through vacuum.

Jarik recoiled, then caught himself. The cat stared back, unblinking.

"Options." Jarik kept his voice level. "I can leave it there and file the weirdest insurance claim in history. Or..."

"You're considering bringing it aboard."

"I'm considering not having whatever-this-is stuck to my ship for the next three jumps."

"It doesn't look distressed."

It didn't. The cat looked mildly inconvenienced—a customer who'd expected better service.

The cat tapped again, pointed at the hull, at itself, made a gesture that said, *Well? Any time now.*

Jarik groaned. "Tractor beam?"

"Operational."

"Will it work on... that?"

"There's only one way to find out."

"I hate this job." Jarik activated the beam. "Targeting forward viewport."

The tractor beam hummed. Through the viewport, pale blue light enveloped the cat. Fur standing on end. Eyes wide. With a sound like bubble wrap popping in a cathedral, it vanished.

"Airlock status?"

"Cycling. Pressurizing. Also—"

The inner airlock door hissed open. Glittering dust poured in, smelling of ozone and something sweet. Through it came the cat, tail high, whiskers forward, tracking stardust across the deck.

It looked at Jarik. Jarik looked at it.

"Hello," the cat said.

His voice was crisp. Precise. Politely condescending.

Also, cats didn't talk. That was a pretty firm rule of biology.

"You..." Jarik's voice trailed off.

"Yes?"

"You... you were in space."

"Briefly." The cat hopped onto the navigation console, scattering coffee droplets. "You really should clean this. It's unsanitary."

"You're a talking cat."

"And you're a pilot who can't navigate. We all have our surprises." The cat examined one paw, licking it thoughtfully. "Also, you did miss the turnoff."

"There IS no turnoff! This is a nebula!"

"A needlessly granular distinction." Those eyes were far too intelligent. "The point is, you're off course. Approximately thirty minutes now."

"How do you—" Jarik shook his head. "You know what? No. I'm not doing this. I'm going to sit here, finish this disaster of a haul, and pretend I hallucinated all of this."

"Mm." The cat stood, stretched, and walked across the console with absolute confidence. Its paws landed on several buttons. None of them looked important. "Is that what you're calling it? Flying into a resonance field?"

"What do you know about resonance fields?"

"Quite a bit, actually. I'm very well-educated." The cat hopped onto the captain's chair—Jarik's chair—and began kneading the cushion. "Unlike some people who take shortcuts through clearly marked hazard zones."

Jarik's hand hovered over the cat, unsure whether to grab it or check his own pulse. "You were floating in vacuum."

"Drifting, technically."

"You should be dead!"

"Should is such a limiting word." The cat settled onto the chair, curling its tail around its paws. "I prefer to focus on what is. And what is, currently, is that you're about to have visitors."

The proximity alarm shrieked again. Jarik spun to the console, where new contacts bloomed across the scanner. Three ships. Five. Seven. Large ones moving in tight formation.

"Please tell me those are friendly," Jarik said.

Val sounded uncertain. "No transponder codes. No identification markers. Energy signatures are—"

"Don't say unusual."

"—running on power sources I don't have in my database."

The cat's ears flattened slightly. Its tail stopped mid-swish. "Ah."

"You know what those are?"

"Unfortunately." The weariness vanished, replaced by practiced nonchalance. "And they know me. I've been avoiding them for three systems now." He looked at Jarik. "You really should learn to recognize an intercept pattern."

"A what?"

"Those ships aren't here for the view."

The lead ship's running lights blazed on. They formed a pattern: a glowing pawprint, rendered in gold, surrounded by symbols that seemed to shift when Jarik looked at them directly.

His stomach dropped. "What is that?"

The cat sighed—an actual, human-sounding sigh. "That is the Familiar Reclamation Bureau of Licensing." It hopped down from the chair and padded toward the cargo bay. "I suggest you start evasive maneuvers. Unless you enjoy paperwork. They have mountains of paperwork."

"The what Bureau? Wait—where are you going?"

"To make myself useful. In theory."

Jarik looked at the console, where a small flame flickered near the spilled coffee. "Don't touch anything!"

"Too late," the cat called back, and pressed a glowing button with its paw.

The ship lurched. The lights cut out. And somewhere deep in the hull, something began making a noise that made Jarik's teeth ache.

In the darkness, lit only by the glow of approaching ships and that ominous golden pawprint, the cat's eyes reflected amber.

Val's voice crackled back to life. "Incoming transmission. They're hailing us."

"Ignore it," Jarik snapped, wrestling with the controls. "Just get the engines back online!"

"Working on it. They're very insistent about the hailing."

The cat hopped back onto the console, settling in like it had all the time in the world. "They'll give you a few minutes before they do anything drastic. Bureaucratic protocols."

Jarik flinched, then forced himself to look at the cat, at the approaching fleet, at his ship's systems struggling to reboot.

"So," the cat said. "You want to know how I got here?"

"Not really!"

"Perfect. I'll start from the beginning."

CHAPTER 2

PASSENGER WITH PAWS

"Beginning of what?" Jarik didn't look up from the console. His fingers flew across the controls, trying to coax the engines back to life. "We don't have time for—"

"It was a Tuesday," the cat said.

"I don't care what day it was!"

"Or possibly a Thursday. Time gets slippery near dimensional rifts."

Jarik slapped the console. A panel sparked, went dark, then flickered back to life. "Val, status!"

"Main power at forty percent and climbing," Val reported. "Engines will be online in approximately four minutes. The Bureau ships are three minutes out."

"That's not good math!"

"I'm aware."

The cat watched Jarik work as if he were an energetic insect. "You're very tense. Have you considered meditation?"

"Have you considered shutting up?"

"Frequently. I reject it on principle." The cat shifted position, taking up more space despite being roughly the size of a small pillow. "I'm Brentley, by the way."

Jarik's hands paused for half a second. "...Brentley?"

"Yes."

"The cat's name is Brentley."

"It's a power name."

"It's a middle-aged accountant name!"

"Precisely." Brentley's tail swished. "No one expects an accountant to steal a starship. It's excellent cover."

"You stole a—" Jarik caught himself. "I don't care. Val, what are those ships doing?"

"Still approaching. Still hailing. New message: 'Surrender the familiar or face immediate impoundment.'"

"What's a familiar?"

Brentley raised one paw, examining his claws. "Technically, I am. Though I prefer 'freelance miracle.' Or 'former deity.' 'Occasional nuisance.' 'That cat from the wanted posters.'"

Jarik looked at him. "Wanted posters?"

"Seventeen systems. It's a personal record."

"Why are you WANTED?"

"Difference of opinion regarding ownership." Brentley yawned, showing far too many teeth. "They think I belong to someone. I think I belong to the concept of freedom itself. We're at an impasse."

Something in the engine room wheezed and clattered, like Val having a coughing fit.

"Val, tell me that was us and not them."

"That was us. The port engine is having an identity crisis."

"Can it have it later?"

"I'll ask."

Jarik dragged a hand through his short, coarse hair. The Bureau ships were getting closer, his engines barely functioning, and there was a talking cat on his console who apparently had a criminal record.

"Alright," he said. "Fine. You're wanted. By these Bureau people. Why?"

"Ah." Brentley settled into a more comfortable position—sprawling across three different controls. "That's where the story gets interesting."

"Val, can you scan him? Figure out what he actually is?"

"Attempting scan now."

Soft blue light washed over Brentley from the ceiling. The cat's fur stood on end. His whiskers vibrated.

Val choked. "That's... that's not possible."

"What?"

"Biological readings are contradictory. Standard Felis Catus, but also something else. Multiple somethings. The classification keeps changing. Also detecting... echoes. Multiple life signatures layered on top of each other. Eight terminated. One active." Val paused. "That shouldn't be possible."

Brentley looked smug. "I contain multitudes."

"Warning," Val continued, sounding strained. "Database match found. Classification: Unregistered familiar. Class Omega. File status: expunged."

"What does expunged mean?"

"It means someone tried very hard to delete all information about him and only partially succeeded. And the records that survive aren't behaving normally. They shift while I read them. One says he was born in the third sector. Another says he was never born at all."

Jarik stared at the cat. The cat stared back, unblinking.

"So you're not just wanted. You're... what? Illegal?"

"Illegal implies I recognize their authority." Brentley licked a paw. "They're simply jealous that I bonded with freedom itself instead of some hedge witch with a cauldron."

"That's not how jealousy works."

"Isn't it?"

The proximity alarm shifted pitch. The Bureau ships were closer now. Jarik could see them through the viewport —sleek white vessels with gold trim and a pawprint symbol glowing on their hulls.

"Two minutes," Val said.

"Engines?"

"Ninety seconds."

Jarik's hands tightened on the controls. "Brentley. I'm going to ask you one more time. Why are they chasing you?"

"Because I escaped."

"From where?"

"From them." Brentley's ears flattened slightly. "Three months ago. Or possibly six. I wasn't keeping a calendar."

"You escaped from—" Jarik gestured at the approaching fleet, "—THEM? How?"

"Cleverness. Luck. A well-timed hairball." The cat's eyes gleamed. "Would you like the full story? It's quite heroic."

"I would like you to tell me how to make them go away!"

"Ah. Well. They won't."

"What?"

"Go away. They're relentless. It's their whole thing." Brentley examined his other paw. "The FRBL doesn't give up. They have a ninety-seven percent recovery rate and never shut up about it. Put it on their letterhead and everything."

His gut clenched. The Bureau had seen Brentley on his ship. They'd chased him. "And the other three percent?"

"Me, mostly."

"Engines online," Val announced. "Barely."

"Shields?"

"What shields?"

"Right." Jarik grabbed the controls. "Hang on to something."

"I'm a cat. I don't need to hang on. I have an innate sense of—" Brentley's words cut off as Jarik threw the ship into a hard turn. Behind him, the small fire on the console still flickered. He'd deal with it later. If there were a later. The cat slid sideways across the console, claws scrabbling for purchase. "—BALANCE!"

The *Marginal Profit* groaned in protest but obeyed, swinging away from the approaching Bureau ships. Through the viewport, Jarik watched the fleet adjust course. They moved in perfect formation, smooth and unhurried.

"They're following us," he said.

"Of course they are. I'm on board."

"Can they track you?"

"Probably. I may have accidentally kept one of their tracking collars." Brentley righted himself, fur standing at odd angles. "It's an excellent neck warmer."

"You're WEARING a tracking device?"

"Wore. Past tense. I removed it near the third moon of Theta Carinae." His ears flattened slightly. "Unfortunately, Class Omega familiars have a certain... signature. We're loud, cosmically speaking. Hard to miss if you know what to listen for."

"So the collar was pointless?"

"The collar was an insult. My objection was philosophical."

Jarik leaned into the controls, pushing for more speed. The ship was gaining momentum, but not enough. The Bureau vessels were faster, cleaner, and built by people who believed in things like "maintenance" and "structural integrity."

"Incoming transmission," Val said. "Text only. It says: 'This is your final warning. Surrender Familiar 7734 immediately.'"

"Familiar 7734?" Jarik glanced at Brentley.

"It's what they call me. I prefer Brentley."

"Final warning means they're about to do something!"

"Yes. Probably activate their tractor beams. Incredibly rude. No sense of personal space." The cat sat down on the captain's chair, his tail curling around his paws. "Though I suppose you'd like to avoid that."

"You suppose correctly!"

"Then you'll need to know how they think. Their procedures. Their weaknesses. Which means you'll need to hear the story."

"I don't need your life story! I need an escape route!"

"Same thing." The cat's eyes caught the light, reflecting green and gold. "You can't outrun them in this ship. It's held together with optimism and spite."

"I'm aware!"

"But you can outthink them. They're bureaucrats to their core. Rules for everything. Procedures for the procedures." Brentley tilted his head. "I should know. I've made them violate most of their protocols at least once."

Jarik's teeth ached. The Bureau vessels were firing something—not weapons, but some kind of energy field that made the hull vibrate at a frequency that shouldn't exist.

"That's the warning shot," Brentley said. "They'll follow with a containment field in approximately thirty seconds."

"How do you know that?"

"Because that's what they always do. Last time, the time before that—." The cat's purr rumbled through the chair. "Greeb's nothing if not predictable."

The surrounding nebula was dense with crystallized stardust—bad for sensors, but maybe good for hiding. If he could find a dense enough patch, lose them in the interference...

"Val, find me the thickest part of the nebula. Somewhere their scanners won't work."

"Searching. Found three candidates. The nearest is forty-five seconds away at current speed."

"Twenty seconds to containment field." Brentley's fur bristled slightly. "Just so you know."

"Can we make it?"

"If the engines don't explode, possibly."

"I'll take possibly!" Jarik adjusted course, pushing the engines harder. The ship protested with new and creative sounds. "Brentley, sit down and shut up."

"I am sitting."

"Then just shut up!"

"But I haven't told you about the abduction yet. That's the important part." The cat kneaded the chair, claws puncturing the worn fabric. "See, it started three months ago. I was napping on a lovely warm engine block—stellar freighter, remarkably cozy, excellent heat distribution—when suddenly—"

The ship lurched. Jarik's stomach dropped as the engines cut out for a full second before roaring back.

"—I was enveloped in the most uncomfortable light," Brentley continued, unbothered. "Utterly rude. I was having the most profound dream about salmon."

"Not now!"

"You did ask how to avoid them."

"I asked for an escape route!"

"And I'm giving you context!" Brentley's tail lashed. "The Bureau captured me once before. Whole containment facility. Security protocols. Guard familiars. The works." His eyes narrowed. "And I escaped. Which means I know how they operate."

The containment field hit.

Lights flickered. Red consoles everywhere. Through the viewport, golden energy spread across the stars—a net of light, reaching.

"Ten seconds to the dense patch," Val said, voice tight.

"We won't make it," Jarik said.

"Not with that attitude." Brentley stood, stretched, and hopped down from the chair. Padded to the console. His ears swiveled forward. "You'll want to reroute power from life support to the engines. Temporarily."

"That'll give us maybe five percent more speed!"

"Five percent is all you need." The cat's paw gestured at a specific button, glowing amber against the console. "That one. Trust me. I've done this before."

Jarik's gaze shifted between the cat, the approaching containment field, and the dense patch of nebula just out of reach. His hand hovered over the controls.

"If I die because I listened to a cat—"

"You won't die. In theory." Brentley's purr took on an edge, almost a growl. "Do you trust me?"

"No!"

"Perfect. Honest foundation for a partnership."

This is insane. The containment field was seconds away. The nebula pocket was right there. But everything about today was insane, and the cat had been right about the warning shot, right about the timing—

He slammed his hand down on the button.

Life support systems whined down. The air thinned. The ship surged forward, engines screaming in protest. Behind them, the containment field grasped at empty space. The *Marginal Profit* dove into the crystallized cloud. The hull sang—a high, keening vibration that made Jarik's fillings ache. Sensors screamed. Through the viewport, crystallized stardust scraped past like frozen lightning.

Free.

For now.

Broken only by alarms and dying systems, the sudden quiet found Jarik slumped in his chair. The small fire on the console had gone out. Finally. An acrid smell lingered, but at least nothing was actively burning.

He stared at his hand, still pressed against the button. *I just became a fugitive. On the advice of a cat I met twenty minutes ago.*

His ship was damaged. The Bureau knew his signature. Even if he surrendered Brentley now, he'd already fled, already resisted—already made his choice.

What have I done?

Brentley hopped back onto the console, looking pleased with himself.

"See?" he said. "Helpful."

"You could have mentioned that thirty seconds ago!"

"Where's the drama in that?" The cat settled down, paws tucked. "Besides, now you know I'm useful. Which means you'll want to hear the rest of the story."

"I want you off my ship!"

"Too late for that. The Bureau knows you're harboring me now. You're complicit. We're in this together. Partners in crime. Comrades in chaos."

"I picked you up ten minutes ago!"

"Time flies when you're fleeing the authorities." The cat's eyes half-closed. "Now. Where was I? Ah yes. The abduction. So there I was, napping peacefully, when the beam hit..."

Jarik opened his mouth to protest, then closed it. The cat was right about one thing—he was complicit now. The Bureau had seen Brentley on his ship. They'd chased him. Which meant even if he ejected the cat into space right now, he'd still be wanted for harboring a fugitive.

And he'd just made it worse by actively fleeing. He looked at Brentley. At the nebula hiding them. At his ship, which had somehow survived another disaster it had no business surviving.

"Fine," he said. "Talk. But make it quick. And tell me something useful."

Brentley's face twisted in what might have been a smile for a cat.

"Oh, it'll be useful. And entertaining. And only mostly true." He settled into a more comfortable position. "It began three months ago, on a warm Tuesday—or Thursday, temporal mechanics get fuzzy—when I was rudely interrupted from the most delightful nap..."

The cat's voice took on a storytelling quality, smooth and

theatrical. And despite everything—the alarms, the danger, the absolute insanity of his situation—Jarik listened.

"I was napping on an engine block. Stellar freighter. Not this one—much nicer. Better coffee." Brentley's eyes gleamed. "The warmth was perfect. The vibrations soothing. And I was having the most profound dream about a salmon the size of a small moon when—"

The ship's lights flickered. Through the viewport, the nebula glittered around them, hiding them from the Bureau ships.

"—when the light came," Brentley said, his voice dropping. "Not sunlight. Not starlight. Something else. Cold and clinical and unbearably official."

Jarik leaned forward despite himself.

"And?" he said.

Brentley's purr rumbled.

"And that," he said, "is when I met Inspector Greeb."

CHAPTER 3

THE ABDUCTION (PROBABLY)

"Greeb," Jarik blinked. "You were captured by someone named *Greeb*?"

"Inspector Greeb," Brentley corrected. "The title is important. Three demotions and a formal reprimand."

"How does that lead to Inspector—"

"Bureaucratic logic. Terribly complex. Very stupid." Brentley waited a beat. "Now, are you going to let me tell this properly, or are you going to interrupt with pedestrian observations about nomenclature?"

Jarik checked the sensors. The Bureau ships were still out there, searching the nebula in a grid pattern. Methodical. Professional. Nothing like the story Brentley was spinning.

"Fine," he said. "Tell it."

"Excellent." Brentley's eyes half-closed, his voice taking on that theatrical quality again. "So. The beam. Cold, white, and utterly devoid of courtesy. One moment I was dreaming of salmon. This salmon had excellent bone structure—sign of a deep thinker—and the next, I was awake and ascending."

"Ascending."

"Against my will. Utterly undignified. My fur was doing that static thing, you know? Where it all stands on end and you look like you've been surprised by existence itself."

Despite himself, Jarik could picture it. "Where were you when this happened?"

"Ah." Brentley considered the question. "That's... somewhat classified."

"Classified by who?"

"Me. I classify my information. It's called privacy." The cat stretched one leg, examining his claws. "Let's say I was on a ship. A nice ship. Much nicer than this one. They had proper heating and coffee that didn't taste like industrial solvent."

"So you were already stowing away on someone else's ship."

"Stowing away implies I was hiding. I was quite visible. I simply wasn't invited." Brentley's purr rumbled. "Anyway. The beam pulled me up through a solid hull—deeply disconcerting, by the way, I don't recommend it—and into their containment hold."

"Just like that? No warning?"

"Oh, there was a warning. An extremely official-sounding voice said 'Unregistered familiar detected. Initiating retrieval protocol.' I chose to ignore it." The cat's ears flattened slightly. "In retrospect, they don't appreciate being ignored."

Jarik checked the sensors. The Bureau ships had spread into a search grid, methodically boxing in different sections of the nebula. Minutes, maybe. Hardly any time at all.

"So you were in their ship," he prompted.

"Indeed." Brentley settled into the memory, voice dropping. "I materialized in what I can only describe as the galaxy's most depressing waiting room. White walls. White floor. White ceiling. Everything was white except for this aggressive golden pawprint on every surface. Very on-brand. Terrible interior design."

"And there were other... familiars?"

"Oh yes. Quite the collection." Brentley's eyes gleamed. "The goldfish to my left looked furious—understandably, given someone had stuffed it into a tiny mechanical suit of brass and copper. A raven sat to my right, large and black, muttering prophecies to itself."

"Muttering what?"

"Prophecies, I assume. It kept saying 'We're all doomed. The universe is uncertain.' Extremely dramatic. Not helpful, but dramatic. And then there was the jar."

"The jar."

"Of mayonnaise. Haunted mayonnaise. The label said 'Dr. Vellum's Sentient Spreads' with a little cartoon blob that seemed to track movement. Deeply unsettling." Brentley said this with complete seriousness. "Just sitting there on a shelf. Glowing slightly. Ominous."

Jarik opened his mouth. Closed it. *Haunted mayonnaise.* He could question it—demand an explanation for how condiments could be possessed, what that even meant in practical terms—but what would be the point? He was being chased by space animal control while a talking cat narrated his own capture. The rules of the universe had clearly taken a vacation.

"Right," he said. "Haunted mayonnaise. Sure."

"I knew you'd understand." Brentley licked a paw. "So there I was, surrounded by the Bureau's latest acquisitions, when the guards arrived."

"More familiars?"

"Correctamundo." The cat's whiskers twitched at his

own word choice. "Dogs, mostly. German Shepherds in little uniforms with badges, looking official and deeply disappointed in all of us." He paused. "There was also an officious raven—different from the muttering one—who kept trying to scan us with this clipboard that glowed."

"A glowing clipboard."

"Enchanted. Clearly. How else would you track magical entities?" Brentley said this as if Jarik was being deliberately obtuse. "The Bureau uses a lot of enchanted office supplies. Paperclips with souls. Staplers that judge you. It's absurdly bureaucratic."

"That doesn't sound real."

"Neither does a talking cat in space, yet here we are, living our best lives." Brentley's purr deepened. "Are you going to keep questioning my lived experience, or shall I continue?"

Jarik waved a hand. "Continue."

"Thank you." The cat resettled himself. "So. The guards were doing their rounds, checking pods, when *he* arrived."

"Greeb."

"Inspector Greeb." Brentley's voice went reverent—mockingly so. "He walked—well, waddled—into the containment area like he owned the place. Which, technically, he did. He was a corgi."

Jarik blinked. "A corgi."

"Yes."

"The inspector was a corgi."

"Pembroke Welsh, if we're being specific. Tan and white. Absurdly fluffy. Extremely serious about his job." Brentley's eyes gleamed with mischief. "He wore a tiny badge on a tiny vest and carried a tiny clipboard under one tiny leg. The effect was meant to be intimidating. It was not."

"But he was in charge?"

"Oh, absolutely. The guards deferred to him immediately. He had an air of—" Brentley paused, searching for words, "—martyred competence. Like he'd been personally victimized by every familiar who'd ever existed, but he was going to process us anyway because someone had to maintain order in this chaotic universe."

Jarik smiled despite himself. "What did he say?"

"He stopped in front of my pod." Brentley's voice went clipped, officious. "'Biological scan complete. Classification: Felis Catus. Status: Unaccompanied. Bonding signature: Absent. Your actions go against Regulation 12-B, which mandates that all familiars without companions must be tagged, neutered, and re-integrated into the narrative.'"

"Narratively re-integrated?"

"Their words, not mine. Sounds rather ominous, doesn't it?" Brentley sounded almost insulted. "I told him good luck with that. I'm quantum declawed."

"What does that even mean?"

"Absolutely nothing." The cat looked pleased with himself. "But Greeb didn't know that. He had to check his clipboard. Twice."

Jarik leaned back in his chair, momentarily distracted from the sensors. Then caught himself. *Why am I listening to this?*

"Then what?"

"The interrogation came next." Brentley took a moment to summon the memory. "He asked me the standard questions. 'What is your designation?' I told him I didn't have one. 'Where is your witch?' I told him I ate her."

"You what?"

"It was a lie, clearly. I've never eaten a witch. Too stringy. All that stress from spell-casting." Brentley groomed a paw casually. "But Greeb wrote it down. Completely straight-faced. 'Familiar consumed practitioner. Note for file.'"

"He believed you?"

"He wrote it down. That's not the same as believing, but it is the same as documenting. Crucial distinction in bureaucracy."

Val's voice crackled through the speakers. "The Bureau ships are tightening their search pattern. They'll reach this section in approximately six minutes."

Jarik's moment of entertainment evaporated. "We need to move."

"In a moment," Brentley said. "This is the important part."

"Your entire story is delays!"

"Context is not delay. Context is essential." The cat's eyes narrowed. "Inspector Greeb stood there with his clipboard and his tiny badge, and he explained—patiently, like he'd done this a thousand times—what the Familiar Reclamation Bureau of Licensing was."

"Which is?"

"An agency dedicated to the recovery, rehabilitation, and rehoming of unaccompanied magical entities." Brentley's voice dripped with disdain. "Their mission statement was literally carved into the wall. 'Every familiar deserves a practitioner. Every practitioner deserves a familiar. We facilitate forever bonds.'"

Jarik's hands stilled on the controls. "Wait. The Familiar Reclamation Bureau?" Something clicked in his memory—late-night stories in dim cargo holds, pilots swapping rumors over cheap beer. "I thought that was a spacer's myth. A ghost story to scare pilots out of picking up weird strays."

"Flattering that they've achieved legendary status." Brentley's tail swished. "But no. Very real. Very persistent. Very fond of paperwork."

"That sounds almost nice," Jarik said weakly, still processing.

"It sounds like a prison with good marketing." Brentley's fur rippled. "They capture familiars whose witches have died, or who've escaped, or who were never bonded in the first place, then 'rehabilitate' us, which means breaking our will and making us compliant before rehoming us with new practitioners."

"But you escaped."

"Of course." The cat's tail swished. "But not immediately. First, I had to understand the system. Learn the procedures. Identify the weaknesses." His eyes gleamed. "And most importantly, I had to figure out who I was dealing with."

"The Bureau."

"Inspector Greeb specifically." Brentley assumed a mock-mournful tone. "He looked at me with these sad little corgi eyes and said, 'I know you think you're special. They all do. But you're not. You're just another unregistered familiar, and you will be processed, rehabilitated, and rehomed. It's for your own good.'"

"What did you say?"

"I said, 'I have transcended the concept of ownership.'" Brentley's whiskers twitched. "He wrote that down too."

A laugh escaped Jarik—once, sharp and short.

The cat looked smug. "See? I told you it was entertaining."

"It's ridiculous."

"Ridiculous and entertaining aren't mutually exclusive." Brentley stood, stretching. "So there I was. Captured. Classified. About to be processed by the galaxy's most persistent animal control agency. The goldfish was still glaring at me. The raven was still prophesying doom. The mayonnaise was still... mayonnaising."

"That's not a verb."

"It is now. I'm very influential." The cat hopped off the console, padding toward the viewport. "And that's when I realized something important."

"What?"

Brentley turned, his eyes reflecting the golden glow from the distant Bureau ships.

"These fools," he said, "had absolutely no idea who they'd captured."

There was a pause. Jarik waited for more. When nothing came, he said, "And who had they captured?"

"Me. Obviously." Brentley's tail swished. "Pay attention."

"That's not an answer!"

"Debatable." The cat's purr rumbled with satisfaction. "I'm Brentley. Unregistered. Uncontained. Unprecedented." He sat down, wrapping his tail around his paws. "And I was already planning my escape."

"How?"

"Well, first I needed to befriend the other prisoners. Build alliances. Establish a network. The goldfish seemed like a good place to start. Anyone who wears a mechanical suit clearly understands the importance of preparation."

"Did you befriend the goldfish?"

"Define befriend."

Before Jarik could respond, Val interrupted. "The Bureau ships are four minutes out. We need to move."

Jarik grabbed the controls. "Hold on."

"I'm a cat. I don't need to—" Brentley's protest cut off as the ship lurched forward, deeper into the nebula. "—hold on. Yes. That. You could have warned me."

"You could have told me a useful story."

"I'm getting to the useful part!" Brentley scrambled back onto the console, claws scratching for purchase. "The escape is the useful part! But you need the setup! You need to understand the facility, the guards, the procedures—"

"What I need is a way to make those ships stop chasing us!"

"And I'm telling you how I did exactly that!" The cat's fur was slightly disheveled now, his dignity ruffled. "If you'd stop interrupting, you'd learn something."

Jarik threw the ship into a sharp turn. The nebula's crystallized dust scraped against the hull with a sound like fingernails on glass.

"Fine," he said. "Keep talking. But talk faster."

Brentley's eyes narrowed. "I don't rush art."

"Rush it or get off my console."

The cat considered this. Then, with a huff that was absolutely indignant, he began again.

"So. The goldfish. His name was Admiral Bubbles..."

CHAPTER 4

PAPERWORK AND PAWPRINTS

"Admiral Bubbles," Jarik repeated, navigating around a dense cluster of crystallized dust. "The goldfish's name was Admiral Bubbles."

"Is. Present tense. He's still alive. Probably." Brentley had returned to his position on the console, looking entirely too comfortable for someone whose story kept getting more absurd. "Unless the Bureau finally caught him. But I doubt it. He's extremely tactical."

"He's a goldfish."

"He's a goldfish in a mechanical combat suit with delusions of naval grandeur." Brentley's tail swished. "There's a difference."

Val's voice crackled. "Bureau ships holding position. They're scanning adjacent sectors."

"How long do we have?"

"Unknown. They're being methodical."

Brentley's whiskers twitched. "That's their whole thing. Methodical. Bureaucratic. Everything by the book." He settled more comfortably. "Which brings me to the tour."

"What tour?"

"The facility tour. Part of processing." Brentley's eyes half-closed, remembering. "After Inspector Greeb finished his little speech about rehabilitation and forever bonds, they moved us from containment to processing. Which meant walking through the entire facility. Remarkably inefficient. But regulations required it."

"Why would regulations require a tour?"

"Regulation 8-D, subsection 4: 'All detained familiars must be shown the full scope of Bureau operations to encourage compliance and discourage future escape attempts.'" Brentley recited this perfectly. "They have a sign about it. Large sign. Gold letters. Extremely official."

Jarik threw him a skeptical look. "You memorized that?"

"I memorize things that amuse me. Bureaucratic overreach is deeply amusing. So. The tour. Picture this: white hallways. Very white. Aggressively white. With gold trim and those pawprint symbols every three meters. And signs. So many signs."

"What kind of signs?"

"'No Loitering.' 'All Familiars Must Be Leashed.' 'Unauthorized Magic Will Be Documented.' 'Report Suspicious Prophecies to Your Nearest Handler.'" Brentley's voice dripped with disdain. "That last one was specifically for ravens. Deeply discriminatory."

"Uh-huh." Jarik checked the sensors again. Still clear. "Go on."

"We walked—well, I walked. Admiral Bubbles rolled in his suit. The raven flew, despite being told not to. The mayonnaise jar was carried by an extremely nervous salamander in a hazmat suit." Brentley paused. "Actually, I'm not sure the salamander was nervous. Salamanders have remarkably limited facial expressions. But he moved like he was nervous."

"About the mayonnaise."

"You would be too if you had to carry haunted condiments through a secure facility." The cat licked a paw. "Anyway. We passed through several sections. The Archives —entire walls of filing cabinets. Enchanted, of course. They glowed purple and occasionally whispered previous cases at you. Extremely distracting."

"Enchanted filing cabinets."

"How else would you store centuries of familiar reclamation data? Regular filing cabinets? Ridiculous." Brentley said this with absolute conviction. "There were also floating paperclips. With souls."

Jarik's hands paused on the controls. "With what?"

"Souls. The paperclips had souls." Brentley examined his claws. "Apparently some witch got creative with a binding spell three hundred years ago, and now the Bureau has sentient office supplies. Ambient magic interacting with mundane technology—happens all the time in places with concentrated magical activity. The Bureau has so many familiars coming through that the background magic just... seeps into things. Makes them aware." His whiskers twitched. "They're very efficient but extremely judgmental. One of them told me my aura was 'unstapled.'"

"Your aura was—"

"Unstapled. I didn't ask for clarification." The cat's tail swished. "We also passed through Records Management, where a depressed-looking phoenix was organizing files alphabetically. Processing, lots of glowing scanners and forms. So many forms. And then Rehabilitation."

"What was Rehabilitation like?"

Brentley's voice went flat. "Terrifying." For the first time, all traces of theatricality vanished. "Rows of pods.

Familiars inside—eyes glowing, repeating phrases. 'I am loyal.' 'I serve willingly.' 'My bond is my purpose.' Over and over."

His gut clenched. The image was too vivid—beings stripped of will, reduced to mantras, their eyes vacant and glowing. *That's what they wanted to do to him.* The thought hit him like cold water. This wasn't just bureaucratic overreach. This was—

"That's—" His hands had stopped moving on the controls. He hadn't noticed. "That's not rehabilitation. That's—"

"Brainwashing?" Brentley's eyes opened fully, meeting Jarik's. "Yes."

Jarik's gaze drifted to the viewport, to the distant glow of the Bureau ships. *They want to do that to him.* The thought sat wrong in his chest—protectiveness for a cat he'd met an hour ago. Ridiculous.

"That's why I needed to escape. The worst part wasn't the pods," Brentley said, his voice still missing its usual theatricality. "It was knowing that somewhere out there, the one I actually—" He stopped. Licked a paw with studied casualness. "Anyway. Processing."

Jarik waited for more. Nothing came. The cat had already moved on, mask back in place.

His hands moved automatically as he adjusted course, keeping them deep in the nebula's interference. But his mind was still in those pods, watching the light in someone's eyes go out and be replaced by something else.

"Processing was where they assigned numbers," Brentley continued, his voice taking on its usual theatrical quality again. "Inspector Greeb walked me—personally, I might add,

I was very important—to this booth. Glass and metal. Scanner built into the floor. He told me to sit on it."

"Did you?"

"Of course not. I sat next to it. He sighed. Picked me up. Placed me on it. I immediately stepped off. We did this four times before he gave up and just activated the scanner while I was nearby."

Despite himself, Jarik smiled. "And?"

"And it worked anyway. Bureau technology is annoyingly effective." The cat's tail lashed. "The scanner lit up, humming—made my teeth ache—before projecting my information in glowing text above the booth."

"What did it say?"

"'Species: Felis Catus. Status: Unregistered. Magical Signature: Class Omega. Practitioner Bond: None. Criminal Record: Extensive. Notes: Subject is difficult.'" Brentley sounded proud of the last part. "Inspector Greeb added a personal note: 'Subject is VERY difficult. Recommend maximum security protocols.'"

"Flattering."

"I thought so." The cat preened slightly. "Next came the pawprint scan. They needed my paw print for their database. Official records. Terribly important."

"Let me guess. You didn't cooperate."

"I cooperated beautifully. I gave them a perfect print." Brentley's eyes gleamed. "Of my left hind paw when they wanted my right front paw."

"That's the same thing."

"Not to the Bureau. The forms specified right front paw in section 3, line 12. I provided the incorrect paw, making the form invalid. We had to start over." The cat's purr rumbled with satisfaction. "We did this six times. Different paws each time."

Jarik actually laughed. "You're terrible."

"Thank you." Brentley accepted this as the compliment it wasn't. "Eventually, Inspector Greeb just scanned all my paws and filed them in quadruplicate. Then he assigned me a number."

The cat's voice shifted, taking on Greeb's clipped tone again. "'You are now Familiar-7734. This designation will be used for all official documentation, rehabilitation sessions, and eventual rehoming paperwork. Welcome to the system.'"

"7734."

"Yes. I told him I had transcended numbering systems. He wrote that down too. 'Subject rejects numerical designation. Possible delusions of grandeur.'" The cat looked pleased. "They are not delusions but accurate assessments."

"Right." Jarik checked the sensors. Still clear. The Bureau ships were searching, but slowly. "So you were in the system. Numbered and scanned. What about the other familiars?"

"Ah yes. My fellow prisoners." Brentley settled into a more comfortable position. "Admiral Bubbles was processed before me. He tried to fight the scanner with his suit's manipulator arms. It didn't work. Utterly tragic. He glared at me the entire time like I should have helped."

"Should you have?"

"I was busy being difficult. Priorities." The cat licked a paw. "The raven—her name was Corvus, I learned later—she cooperated completely. She stepped onto the scanner and provided clear identification. She even answered questions."

"Sounds reasonable."

"It sounds suspicious." Brentley's eyes narrowed. "No self-respecting raven cooperates that easily. I knew immediately she was planning something."

Jarik's skepticism must have shown on his face, because Brentley's tail lashed.

"She was! She looked at me while they were scanning her and said, 'The chaos comes on swift wings.' Extremely ominous, deeply prophetic, and clearly a coded message."

"Or she was just being a raven."

"Same thing." Brentley dismissed this. "And then there was the mayonnaise."

"What about the mayonnaise?"

"They tried to scan it. The jar or whatever was inside." Brentley paused. "The scanner exploded."

"Exploded?"

"Well. It sparked, made a terrible sound, and shut down completely. Inspector Greeb stared at it for a full minute before writing on his clipboard: 'Subject 8854-M declined processing. Recommend quarantine.' And they simply moved on."

"They gave up on the mayonnaise."

"Even the Bureau has limits." Brentley's purr rumbled. "After processing, they assigned us temporary quarters. 'Rehabilitation pods,' they called them. Small rooms with white walls and glowing restraints. There was a food dispenser that produced the galaxy's saddest kibble and a speaker that played affirmations on loop."

"Affirmations?"

"'You are safe here. Bonding is beautiful. Resistance is loneliness.'" Brentley's voice dropped. "On a loop, twenty-four hours. I couldn't turn it off."

"That sounds—"

"Effective? Yes. That's the word you keep using." The cat's eyes gleamed. "But it also meant they underestimated us. They thought the affirmations and the kibble and the glowing restraints would break our will. Make us compliant."

"And it didn't?"

"Please. I've been ignoring humans telling me what to do for years. A speaker doesn't intimidate me." Brentley stood, stretching. "So I started planning. I made contact with Admiral Bubbles through the ventilation system. It had surprisingly good acoustics but terrible security."

"And he helped you escape?"

"Eventually. First, we had to establish trust which was difficult because he blamed me for his capture."

Jarik blinked. "Why would he blame you?"

"He said something about me stealing his warm spot on that stellar freighter? I don't remember. It was water under the bridge." Brentley waved a paw dismissively. "The point is, we agreed to work together. He had the technical knowledge—mechanical suit, remember—and I had the charisma."

"The charisma."

"Leadership qualities. Vision. The ability to inspire others to take risks they wouldn't normally take." The cat's tail swished. "That's essential in any escape attempt."

Val interrupted. "Bureau ships are moving. They're expanding their search pattern."

"How long?" Jarik asked.

"Two minutes until they reach this sector."

Jarik swore softly and adjusted course again, pushing

deeper into the nebula. The *Marginal Profit* groaned but obeyed.

"You're going to want to hear the rest of this," Brentley said calmly. "The escape is relevant to your current predicament."

"My current predicament is listening to a cat tell an increasingly implausible story while being hunted by space animal control!"

"See? You're learning. Now. Where was I? Ah yes. Corvus."

"The raven."

"The raven who claimed she was on my side. She said her prophecies told her we'd escape together, that I was 'the catalyst of chaos' and she was 'the wings of witnessing.'" Brentley paused. "It was very dramatic. Typical for ravens."

"Did she help you escape?"

"Define help."

Jarik shot him a look. "Are we doing this again?"

"It's a legitimate question! Help is subjective. Did she assist in my escape? Yes. Did she betray me to the guards first? Also yes." Brentley's tail lashed. "It's complicated."

"Wait." Jarik's hands paused on the controls. "You said earlier she was your ally."

"She was."

"But now you're saying she betrayed you."

"She did both. It's called multi-tasking." Brentley licked a paw, completely unconcerned.

"That's not how multi-tasking works!"

"Isn't it?" The cat looked up with those too-intelligent eyes. "She warned the guards I was planning something. But she also left the ventilation grate unlocked. Betrayal and assistance. Both happened."

"That's—" Jarik searched for words. "That's a contradiction."

"No, no. She prophesied about me. Entirely different." Brentley said this with absolute confidence. "Ravens deal in prophecy. Sometimes helping looks like hindering. It's all terribly mystical and confusing, but ultimately useful."

"That makes no sense."

"Prophecy rarely does." The cat settled back down. "The point is, between Admiral Bubbles's technical expertise, Corvus's strategic betrayal-slash-assistance, and my natural brilliance, we started forming a plan."

"What kind of plan?"

"The kind that involved stolen catnip, a reflective bowl, and several poor decisions." Brentley's eyes gleamed. "But I'm getting ahead of myself. First, the daily routine. Rehabilitation sessions twice a day. Extremely tedious."

"What happened in rehabilitation?"

"They'd take us to a room. A white room. Surprise. And make us practice bonding with temporary practitioners. Junior Bureau agents learning their trade, nervous humans holding treats and trying to establish 'magical connections.'"

"Did it work?"

"On some familiars, yes. The goldfish refused. Corvus pretended to cooperate but gave terrible prophecies. 'I foresee your paperwork multiplying.' 'The audit comes on silent wings.' That sort of thing." The cat's purr rumbled with amusement. "It made the trainees extremely uncomfortable."

"And you?"

"I was perfectly charming. I purred and accepted the treats. I even did a few tricks." Brentley paused. "Before knocking over their spell components and blaming it on quantum instability."

"There's no such thing as—"

"They didn't know that. Bureau training is heavily focused on procedure, not physics." The cat looked smug. "I got flagged as 'magically unstable' and moved to a higher security pod, which was exactly what I needed."

"Why would you want higher security?"

"It had a better ventilation system with larger grates and more escape routes." Brentley's whiskers twitched. "The Bureau's obsession with security makes them predictable. They put all the 'difficult' familiars in the same section, which means all the familiars most likely to escape were suddenly in close proximity. It was shockingly poor planning on their part."

Despite his better judgment, Jarik was listening. "So you were all together."

"In adjacent pods, yes. Me. Admiral Bubbles. Corvus. Even the mayonnaise—though it remained ominously silent." The cat's eyes gleamed. "And that's when the proper planning began."

"One minute," Val announced. "Bureau ships entering this sector."

Jarik's hands tightened on the controls. "Brentley—"

"I know, I know. Time is short. You need answers." The cat stood, stretching. "But you need to understand: the Bureau is patient and methodical. They'll search every square meter of this nebula until they find us. Unless—"

"Unless what?"

"Unless we do something they don't expect. Something chaotic. Something that breaks their procedures."

"Like what?"

"Like what I did before." The cat's tail swished again. "The Bureau thought they could contain me. Rehabilitate me and make me compliant." His eyes caught the light, reflecting green and gold. "But I had a plan."

"Did you?" Jarik couldn't help asking. "Actually have a plan?"

Brentley's whiskers twitched.

"I had the *concept* of a plan," he said. "Close enough."

CHAPTER 5

THE GREAT ESCAPE

"The concept of a plan," Jarik said, keeping one eye on the sensors where the Bureau ships crept closer, "is not an actual plan."

"I disagree. Concepts are the foundation of all grand plans." Brentley's tail swished. "Also, I had supplies. Three stolen catnip packets from the rehabilitation sessions. A reflective bowl from the cafeteria. And several bad intentions."

"That's not a plan. That's a grocery list for disaster."

"Exactly." The cat's purr rumbled with satisfaction. "The Bureau expects plans. Careful coordination. Logical steps. They don't expect inspired chaos."

"Thirty seconds," Val warned. "Bureau ships are extremely close now."

Jarik threw the ship into another turn, buying them time. "Talk faster."

"Fine. No artistry, only facts." Brentley stood, pacing across the console. "On day seventeen of captivity, I'd made contact with Admiral Bubbles through the vents. He'd been working on his suit's articulation—apparently the Bureau's restraints interfered with his manipulator arms. Extremely frustrating for him."

"I'm sure."

"Don't be dismissive. He was the key to the entire operation." The cat's eyes gleamed. "Corvus had been having prophetic episodes in her pod. Loud ones. 'The locks will fail! The doors will open! The mayonnaise will—' well, that one was unclear. But it got the guards' attention."

"How is that helpful?"

"Because while they were distracted by her prophesying, I was picking the lock on my pod with a stolen paperclip." Brentley said this casually, like lock-picking was a perfectly normal cat skill.

"The paperclips with souls?"

"The very same. This one was named Gerald. He was remarkably helpful and deeply dissatisfied with his career path. Kept muttering about transferring to Accounting where at least the staplers had retirement plans." The cat's whiskers twitched. "I promised him freedom if he helped me. He agreed, so we jimmied the lock together."

Jarik wanted to point out that cats don't have opposable thumbs, but he was fairly certain Brentley would have an answer for that too.

"So you got out of your pod," he said instead.

"I did. It was the middle of the night cycle with minimal guard presence. Excellent timing." Brentley's tail lashed with the memory. "First stop: Admiral Bubbles. His lock was more complex—mechanical suit, so different security protocols—but Gerald was motivated. We got him out."

"Then what?"

"Admiral Bubbles rolled out of his pod in full combat mode. Manipulator arms extended and tiny forward-mounted lasers active. He looked absolutely ridiculous and completely unstoppable." The cat's purr deepened. "He said, and I quote, 'Time to teach these mammals some respect.'"

"The goldfish said that."

"He has a voice synthesizer in the suit. Incredibly tinny, but yes." Brentley hopped down from the console, acting out the scene. "We moved to Corvus's pod next. She was already awake. She said she'd foreseen our arrival."

"Had she?"

"Probably not, but it's what ravens do. They pretend they predicted everything." The cat's tail swished. "She hopped onto my back—very undignified, by the way—and we headed for the mayonnaise."

"Why the mayonnaise?"

"Honestly? I'm still not sure." Brentley paused. "But Corvus insisted saying it was 'narratively essential.' And she was right."

"Fifteen seconds," Val announced.

Jarik's hands flew across the controls. "Brentley—"

"Almost done. This is the important part." The cat's voice quickened. "We reached the mayonnaise's pod. Gerald picked that lock too—he was really getting into it by now, questioning his entire existence as office supplies. And when the door opened, the jar just... sat there... all glowing and ominous."

"Did you take it?"

"Admiral Bubbles grabbed it with his manipulator arm with extreme care. The moment he touched it, every alarm in the facility went off." Brentley's eyes gleamed. "Apparently haunted mayonnaise is classified as a Class-7 Reality Hazard. So, removing it from its containment pod triggered automatic lockdown protocols."

"That sounds bad."

"It was excellent. Chaos was everywhere. Guards were scrambling, automated defenses activating, and us running through the corridors with a goldfish in a mech suit carrying cursed condiments." The cat's purr rumbled with delight. "It was poetry in motion."

Through the viewport, the nearest Bureau ship's running lights blazed. Too close.

"What happened next?" he asked, despite himself.

"Inspector Greeb showed up, of course." Brentley's voice took on that mocking quality again. "He came waddling around the corner in his tiny vest, looking absolutely betrayed. 'Familiar-7734! You will return to your pod immediately! Regulation 45-C clearly states—'"

"He was quoting regulations while you were escaping?"

"He's extremely dedicated to procedure." The cat's tail lashed. "I told him I'd transcended pod-based living. He wrote that down before trying to activate a containment field."

"Did it work?"

"On Corvus, yes. She got trapped in a glowing bubble and started prophesying dramatically. 'The chaos! The chaos comes!' Extremely helpful." Brentley paused. "Admiral Bubbles shot the generator with his tiny laser, but the generator was apparently quite delicate. The containment field popped like a soap bubble."

"And Greeb?"

"Inspector Greeb chased us through the corridors. Relentlessly determined. Those corgi legs can really move when motivated." Brentley's claws extended slightly at the memory.

"The hallways weren't designed for high-speed pursuits though. There were lots of low doorways. Inspector Greeb kept having to duck. He lost his clipboard twice. Deeply undignified."

Despite everything, Jarik grinned. "Where were you going?"

"The hangar, clearly. We needed a ship." The cat's eyes gleamed. "But first, I needed a distraction, which is where the catnip came in."

"The stolen catnip."

"The strategically acquired catnip, yes." Brentley hopped back onto the console. "I'd crushed it into powder and mixed it with the reflective dust from the bowl. I made little packets. Highly volatile, but extremely effective on most mammalian species."

"You made catnip grenades."

"I made tactical distraction devices." The cat looked smug. "I threw them at the pursuing guards. Three dog familiars, two cat familiars, and one thoroughly confused ferret. The effect was immediate."

"They were affected by catnip."

"Powerfully affected. Suddenly everything was fascinating. The walls. The ceiling. Their own paws." Brentley's purr rumbled. "The ferret tried to arrest a door. The cats started a fight over a dust particle. The dogs forgot they were guards and started playing. Wonderfully distracting."

"What about Greeb?"

"Corgis are surprisingly resistant to catnip. He kept coming." The cat's tail twitched. "But he was alone now and we had Admiral Bubbles, who was fiercely protective of the mayonnaise. I still don't know why. They'd bonded somehow."

"The goldfish bonded with the haunted mayonnaise."

"Stranger things have happened. You picked up a cat in space today." Brentley said this as if it were perfectly logical. "Anyway, we reached the hangar. There were multiple ships giving us multiple options. I chose a small courier vessel with good engines and terrible security."

"How did you know how to fly it?"

"I didn't, but Admiral Bubbles did. Apparently his previous practitioner was a pilot. He plugged into the navigation system. Corvus took the copilot seat and started prophesying coordinates. The mayonnaise... sat there. Still glowing."

"And you?"

"I sat in the captain's chair, naturally. It was my escape." Brentley's eyes gleamed. "That's when Inspector Greeb arrived. He ran into the hangar and tried to stop us. It was incredibly brave, but utterly futile."

"What did you do?"

"I told him this wasn't personal and that I appreciated his dedication to procedure. However, he was simply on the wrong side of freedom." The cat paused. "Admiral Bubbles activated the engines and we blasted a hole in the hangar door."

Jarik blinked. "You what?"

"It was a small hole. Maybe a medium hole. The size was never officially determined." Brentley waved a paw dismissively. "But it was large enough to fly through. And small enough to claim it was an accident."

"That's not—"

"It was a tragic paperwork accident. Happens all the time." The cat's tail swished. "The important thing is, we escaped. We shot out of the hangar through the hole and into beautiful, empty space."

"All of you?"

"Well. Admiral Bubbles and the mayonnaise made it to the ship—"

"Wait," Jarik interrupted. "You said Corvus was in the copilot seat."

"Did I? I meant she was *heading* for the copilot seat. But then she flew out under her own power instead. Wings, you know. Extremely convenient." The cat's tail twitched. "Highly symbolic. Where was I?"

"You were lying."

"I was establishing narrative flow. Anyway, I may have miscalculated the trajectory slightly." The cat's voice lost its theatrical edge. "I was ejected from the ship during the initial thrust."

Brentley's ears flattened. His eyes went distant—not performing now, not playing for laughs. Just a cat who'd watched the only beings who'd helped him disappear into the stars.

Then he blinked, and the mask snapped back into place. "It was extremely dramatic and unexpected."

Jarik stared at him. "You were thrown out of your own escape ship."

"Ejected implies a loss of control. I prefer to think of it as an unplanned trajectory adjustment." Brentley's purr rumbled defensively. "I tumbled through space quite gracefully. The stars wheeling around me. The Bureau facility growing smaller behind me. The ship with Admiral Bubbles and Corvus disappearing in the distance."

"They left you?"

"They didn't know I'd been ejected. Communication systems weren't online yet." The cat's tail lashed. "So there I was. Drifting and alone in the hard vacuum of space with nothing but my natural charm and inexplicable survival skills."

"For three months?"

"For however long it took to drift from there to here." Brentley's eyes narrowed. "Time gets weird in space. Also, I may have been in stasis. Or napping. The distinction is unclear."

"That makes no sense."

"Neither does surviving vacuum. Yet here I am." The cat settled back down. "And that's how I ended up on your windshield. Destiny. Fate. Poor navigation on your part."

Jarik opened his mouth to protest the complete absurdity of everything he'd just heard when Val's voice cut through the cabin.

"Warning. Large vessel approaching. Familiar Reclamation Bureau of Licensing signature detected."

Both of them froze.

Slowly, Jarik turned to look at the sensors. There, emerging from the nebula's interference like a shark through murky water, was a ship.

His pilot's instincts catalogued it automatically: *Leviathan-class enforcement frigate. Military-grade shielding. Weapons arrays that could vaporize a moon. Crew complement of three hundred, minimum.*

The *Marginal Profit* was a rust bucket held together with hope. That thing was a flying fortress.

"Val," his voice came out steady through sheer force of will, "escape vectors. Now."

"Calculating." A pause. "There are none."

"Calculate harder!"

"The physics don't change because you're upset about them."

A massive ship of white and gold filled the viewport. Spotless. That glowing pawprint symbol bright enough to hurt. It was shaped as if someone had combined a litter box with a courthouse and made it fly.

And it was close enough that Jarik could see individual hull plates.

"Jump coordinates," he said, hands already moving. "Anywhere. I don't care where—"

"Jump drive requires ninety seconds to charge. They'll have us in a tractor beam in forty."

Jarik's mind raced through options, discarding each one as quickly as it formed. Couldn't outrun them. Couldn't outgun them. Couldn't hide—they were already spotted. Could try to—no, that wouldn't work either. The nebula was too thin here. If he went deeper he'd lose the engines to crystallized buildup before—

Brentley's purr stopped. "Oh. They upgraded."

"That's the Bureau?" Jarik's voice came out higher than intended.

"That's the Bureau." The cat's tail had gone completely still. "They didn't have that ship three months ago. Or whenever I escaped. Time is still unclear."

The vessel filled the viewport now, dwarfing the *Marginal Profit*.

"They're hailing us," Val said.

Neither of them moved.

"They're quite insistent about the hailing," Val added.

Jarik's hands didn't stop moving across the controls. "Val, what if we vent the cargo bay? Use the explosive decompression to—"

"Insufficient thrust. They'd compensate in three seconds."

"The port stabilizer. If I overload it—"

"You'd destroy the stabilizer and gain nothing."

"There has to be—" He slammed the console. "There has to be *something*!"

Jarik looked at Brentley. "Your story about escaping, about the paperwork accident and the hole in the hangar—"

"Yes?"

"That was all true?"

"Define true."

"BRENTLEY!"

"The broad strokes were accurate! I may have exaggerated certain details for dramatic effect—"

The proximity alarm joined the hailing alert. The overlapping sounds made Jarik's teeth ache.

"—but yes, fine, I escaped from them heroically with some help. And possibly more luck than skill." The cat's ears flattened slightly. "The point is, they're extremely motivated to get me back."

Jarik looked at the massive Bureau ship. The cat. His own poor life choices lined up in a row.

"That story made no sense," he said.

"Yet here we are living it. Reality makes no sense. I've simply embraced that."

"That's not even—" Jarik cut himself off. "We're going to die because I picked up a cat who destroyed government property and is now wanted by an entire cosmic agency."

"Technically, the mayonnaise destroyed the hangar. I just facilitated." Brentley's tail twitched. "Also, we're not going to die. In theory."

The hailing alert reached a new pitch of urgency.

"Answer it," Brentley said quietly. "They won't shoot until they've filed the proper forms. Bureaucratic protocols. We have time."

"Time for what?"

Brentley turned, his eyes reflecting the golden glow from the distant Bureau ships.

"Time," he said, "for me to think of an actual plan."

Through the viewport, the massive Bureau ship began powering weapons systems.

CHAPTER 6

A DISTURBANCE
IN THE BUREAU

"Answer it," Jarik said, reaching for the communication panel. His hand shook slightly. "Maybe we can—"

"Lie?" Brentley suggested. "Negotiate? Plead ignorance?"

"Any of those!"

"It won't work. They've already scanned the ship. They know I'm here." The cat's tail twitched. "But sure. Answer it. Might as well be polite about our impending capture."

Jarik stabbed the communication button. Static crackled through the speakers, then cleared.

"Attention unidentified vessel." The voice was crisp, professional, and carried the authority that came from filing things in triplicate. "This is the FRBL Enforcement Vessel Perpetual Compliance. You are harboring a Class-Omega escaped familiar. Please power down your engines and prepare for boarding."

Jarik looked at Brentley. Brentley looked at his paws.

"Hello?" the voice continued. "We know you can hear us. Your communication systems are active. Ignoring a Bureau hail violates Regulation 3-A and will be noted in your permanent record."

"They have permanent records on everyone," Brentley muttered. "Very thorough."

Jarik unmuted the channel. "This is the cargo hauler *Marginal Profit*. There's been a misunderstanding. I'm just passing through—"

"Ship registration confirmed. Captain: Jarik Venn. Current cargo: freeze-dried rations, replacement parts, and one unregistered familiar." The voice paused. "The familiar is our primary concern. Please surrender them peacefully."

"Them?" Brentley's ears perked up. "They don't even know my gender. Sloppy."

"It," the voice corrected, clearly having heard that. "The familiar. Entity designation Familiar-7734, also known as—" there was a sound like pages turning, "—Brentley. Also known as The Whisker Menace. Also known as Project Persistence. Also known as That Damned Cat."

"I prefer Brentley," Brentley said loudly.

Silence on the other end. Then a voice came through. "Brentley. We know it's you."

The cat's tail went still. "You'll have to be more specific. I've escaped a lot of things."

"Three months ago, you destroyed Bureau property. Compromised a secure facility. Released multiple contained entities. And caused approximately fifty thousand credits worth of damage." The voice had taken on a personal quality now. Less professional. More annoyed. "Do you remember me, Brentley?"

"Inspector Greeb?"

"Enforcement Director Greeb now. I was promoted after your escape." The voice dripped with satisfaction. "They wanted someone with... personal experience... to lead the recovery efforts."

"Congratulations on the promotion."

"It came with a fifty percent increase in paperwork and a mandatory therapy stipend." Greeb's voice hardened. "Surrender now, and I'll note your cooperation in the official report."

Brentley looked at Jarik. Jarik looked at the massive Bureau ship blocking their escape route.

"What happens if we don't?" Jarik asked.

"We activate tractor beams, board your vessel by force, and charge you with harboring a fugitive familiar. You'll be fined, your ship will be impounded, and you'll spend the next six months filling out forms." Greeb paused. "In triplicate."

"That's not even a real threat," Jarik said.

"You haven't seen the forms." Greeb sounded genuinely serious about this. "Ever since the Unification Accords forced us to integrate magical and mundane law, the paperwork has become impossible. Form 2847-B alone requires seventeen separate signatures, three from certified magical witnesses, two from non-magical authorities, and a notarized statement of intent verified by both systems."

Jarik's hand hovered over the engine controls. The *Marginal Profit* was no match for the Bureau ship. That much was obvious. The *Perpetual Compliance* didn't have a single dent, scorch mark, or questionable stain. An unlimited budget would do that. Its hull was pristine white with gold trim. Weapon ports lined its sides. And the pawprint symbol glowed across its bow like a warning.

"Val. Analysis."

Val's voice crackled. "Bureau vessel specs: Heavy frigate class. Magical shielding at ninety-eight percent. Conventional shields at maximum. Weapons systems active.

Tractor beam warming up." A pause. "We cannot outrun it. We cannot outgun it. We probably cannot out-bureaucracy it."

"Probably?"

"Brentley might. But statistically unlikely."

The cat's ears flattened slightly. "You actually escaped from THEM?" Jarik gestured at the massive ship. "From that?"

"Well." Brentley's tail twitched. "Not from that ship specifically. From a facility. It's different."

"How is that different?"

"The facility was stationary. It's easier to escape from stationary things." The cat's voice had lost some of its usual confidence. "Also, they've clearly upgraded their pursuit protocols since my escape."

"You think?"

"In my defense, I was excellent at escaping. Past tense." Brentley hopped down from the console, padding toward the viewport. "Present tense is still being determined."

The *Perpetual Compliance* drifted closer. Jarik could see smaller details now—sensor arrays that tracked their every movement, docking ports that looked sturdy enough to breach a hull, and what might have been enchanted restraints mounted on external hardpoints.

"You have thirty seconds to respond," Greeb's voice announced. "After which we will assume hostile intent and act accordingly."

"Hostile intent?" Jarik's voice cracked slightly. "I picked up a hitchhiker!"

"A wanted hitchhiker with extensive property damage charges and possible reality alteration violations." Greeb sounded like he was reading from a list. "We have evidence of at least three separate incidents where probability shifted in his vicinity."

"That was never proven," Brentley said.

"The containment pod exploded in a room with no explosives while you were inside it. Alone."

"Coincidence."

"The odds were calculated at one in four billion."

"I'm very lucky." The cat's tail lashed. "It's not a crime to be lucky."

"It is when you're a Class-Omega familiar with reality manipulation tendencies." Greeb's voice took on a lecturing quality. "Do you know how much paperwork a reality fluctuation generates? Do you?"

"Is it more or less than the paperwork for a hangar door?"

"Twenty seconds," Greeb said, ignoring that. "I'm trying to be reasonable here, Brentley. Cooperate now, and the charges will be limited to escape and property damage. Resist, and we add obstruction, reality tampering, and corrupting a civilian vessel operator."

Jarik's head whipped around. "Corrupting?"

"It's a technical term," Brentley said. "Means you helped me. Even accidentally."

"I didn't help you! You hit my windshield!"

"And you brought me aboard. Gave me shelter. You allowed me to tell my story without interruption—"

"I interrupted constantly!"

"Insufficiently. According to Bureau regulations, any assistance rendered to an escaped familiar, intentional or otherwise, constitutes harboring. You're an accessory."

"To what? Bad luck?"

"To my continued freedom." Brentley hopped back onto the console. "Which, granted, looks increasingly temporary."

"Ten seconds," Greeb announced.

Jarik's mind raced. He could try to run—push the engines past their safety limits, hope the nebula's interference bought them time. But Val had already calculated those odds. They were not good.

He could surrender—hand over the cat, file the forms, pay the fines.

But his ship would still be impounded. The fines would still bankrupt him. He'd still lose everything trying to prove he was just an innocent bystander. The Bureau didn't care about innocent. They cared about documentation and compliance.

Either way, he lost.

Unless.

At least if he fought, it would be his choice. His ship. His decision. Not theirs.

The thought settled in his chest like cold metal. *If I'm going down anyway, I'm going down on my own terms.*

"This is insane," he muttered.

"Most good decisions are." Brentley's eyes gleamed. "Your call, captain."

"Five seconds."

Jarik took a breath. Let it out. Made a decision he'd probably regret.

"Might as well answer it properly," he said, unmuting the channel. "Inspector—sorry, Director Greeb. This is Captain Venn. We're... we're not surrendering."

Silence. Then a voice came back. "I was afraid you'd say that."

"In my defense—"

"There is no defense for harboring an escaped familiar." Greeb sounded more tired than angry. "I'm activating tractor beams now. Please don't try anything clever. The last three vessels that tried something clever are still doing community service."

"Community service?"

"Picking up space debris in the Theta Sector. Extremely tedious assignment. Multi-year contracts with no early termination clause." Greeb paused. "I'm giving you one final chance. Open your airlock. Let me board. We'll process everything properly and minimize the charges."

Brentley's tail poofed slightly. "He's being unusually reasonable. That's suspicious."

"Or he's trying to avoid more property damage," Jarik said.

"Same thing."

The tractor beam activated. A pale blue field enveloped the *Marginal Profit*, and Jarik felt the controls go sluggish.

It was like hands closing around his throat.

The ship—*his* ship—wasn't responding to him anymore. The yoke pulled against his grip, dragged by invisible force. The *Marginal Profit* had been his for six years. Through three crash landings, two failed relationships, and a thousand lonely jumps. It wasn't much, but it was *his*.

And now someone else was flying it.

His hands tightened on controls that no longer obeyed him. The violation of it burned through his chest—not fear, but something fiercer. Anger. Defiance.

Mine.

"Tractor beam active," Val confirmed. "We're being pulled toward their docking port."

"Can you break free?"

"Not without tearing the ship apart. Also no."

Jarik slumped in his chair, watching through the viewport as the *Perpetual Compliance* grew larger. Its docking port irised open, revealing a pristine airlock bathed in that clinical white light.

"Well," Brentley's tail went still. "This is unfortunate."

"Unfortunate? UNFORTUNATE?" Jarik's voice climbed an octave. "I'm being arrested by space animal control because a cat told me a ridiculous story!"

"A mostly true story."

"THAT'S WORSE!"

Magnetic clamps engaged with a clang, locking them in place. Through the viewport, Jarik could see figures moving in the Bureau airlock. Uniforms. Clipboards. An officious-looking raven with a badge.

"They're boarding us, aren't they?" he said, defeated.

Brentley watched the preparations with professional interest. "Yes. But look—this is excellent material for my memoirs."

Jarik turned to stare at him. "Your memoirs."

"Chapter Seven: The Daring Rescue That Wasn't. Quite dramatic. You'll come across remarkably heroic in it."

"I didn't do anything heroic!"

"You didn't surrender immediately. That's practically heroism by Bureau standards." The cat's purr rumbled. "Most people hand me over within five minutes. You lasted—" he glanced at an imaginary timepiece, "—almost an hour. Very impressive."

"An hour of my life I'll never get back."

"An hour of excellent storytelling and character development." Brentley hopped down, padding toward the airlock. "Now. When they board, let me do the talking."

"Absolutely not."

"I have experience with Bureau protocols."

"Your experience got us INTO this mess!"

"And it might get us out." The cat's eyes gleamed. "Statistically speaking. But maybe not. The distinction is important."

A metallic clang echoed through the ship as the Bureau's airlock connected with theirs. Pressurization hissed. Locks engaged with final, inevitable clicks.

Val's voice was apologetic. "They're opening our outer airlock door."

Jarik stood, hands clenched at his sides. Beside him, Brentley sat down, wrapped his tail around his paws, and looked remarkably calm for someone about to be recaptured by the agency he'd escaped from three months ago.

"How are you so calm?" Jarik asked.

"Practice. Also, denial. Mostly denial."

The inner airlock door hissed open.

And through it walked Inspector—Enforcement Director—Greeb.

He was, in fact, a corgi. Tan and white, fluffy, with dark intelligent eyes and an extremely serious expression. He wore a vest with the Bureau's pawprint symbol embroidered in gold thread. A badge hung from it, gleaming. And tucked under one foreleg was a clipboard, faintly glowing.

Behind him came two more familiars. An owl—large, grey, stern-faced, wearing tactical armor adapted for avian physiology. One eye was scarred shut. And a rabbit—white, red-eyed, twitching with barely contained energy, holding what might have been a stunner or possibly just a weaponized carrot. It was hard to tell.

Greeb stepped onto the deck plating, set down his clipboard, and sighed. His nose twitched. "Is something burning?"

"Minor electrical fire," Jarik said. "It's under control."

"It doesn't smell under control."

"It's *mostly* under control."

"Brentley," he said. "It's been three standard cycles."

The cat's tail twitched. "Has it? Time is so fluid when you're cosmically significant."

"Three months, two weeks, and four days." Greeb's voice was flat. "I've been tracking it. They made me track it. There's a countdown in the main office."

"How's it look?"

"Depressing. But accurate." The corgi picked up his clipboard, glancing at it. "You destroyed a hangar door. Released three contained entities. Compromised our security protocols. And cost the Bureau enough in repairs that I had to attend six budget meetings."

"My condolences on the meetings."

"They were excruciating." Greeb looked up, fixing Brentley with those dark eyes. "Do you know how many forms I've filled out because of you?"

"More than zero?"

"Two thousand, four hundred, and seventy-three." He'd counted every single one. "Each one requiring multiple signatures, notarization, and witnesses."

"That does sound tedious."

"It was soul-crushing." Greeb turned to Jarik. "And you must be the unfortunate civilian who picked him up."

"I—" Jarik started.

"Don't answer that. It's rhetorical." The corgi consulted his clipboard. "Captain Jarik Venn. Freelance hauler. Clean record until approximately—" he checked, "—an hour ago when you rescued an escaped Class-Omega familiar from open space."

"He hit my windshield!"

"And you brought him aboard." Greeb made a note. "That's harboring. Form 2847-B. We'll need your statement, your ship's logs, and a formal declaration of intent."

"I didn't intend anything! He was in space!"

"Intent is assumed upon rescue." The corgi's voice was matter-of-fact. "Regulation 15-D is quite explicit on this matter. You had options—ignore him, report him, maintain distance. You chose retrieval."

"He would have—" Jarik stopped. "Actually, I don't know what would have happened. He was fine in vacuum."

"Exactly." Greeb made another note. "Which should have been your first warning that this was a Bureau matter."

Brentley's tail lashed. "Are you done lecturing? It's just that we have places to be. Freedom to maintain. The usual."

Greeb turned back to him. The corgi's expression shifted from tired bureaucrat to something harder.

"You're not going anywhere. By authority of FRBL Code Section 9, Subsection 4—" Greeb's voice took on that rehearsed quality, "—Paragraph 12, I'm placing you under formal containment pending rehabilitation review."

"Rehabilitation is such an ugly word."

"It's the correct word." Greeb nodded to the owl and

rabbit. "Prepare standard restraints. Magical and physical. He's resourceful."

The enforcement familiars moved forward. The owl produced a collar from somewhere in its armor—glowing softly, inscribed with symbols that hurt to look at. The rabbit held what was definitely not a carrot but some kind of stunner device.

Brentley's fur rippled. "I should mention, I have a medical exemption for neck accessories."

"You don't." Greeb consulted his clipboard. "Your file lists no medical conditions, exemptions, or special accommodations. Though there is a note here that says 'Subject claims quantum declawing. Unverified.'"

"I stand by that statement."

"It's meaningless." The corgi's ears twitched. "Are you going to cooperate? Or do we need to do this the difficult way?"

"I wasn't aware there was a cooperative way to be imprisoned."

"There's efficient imprisonment and there's complicated imprisonment." Greeb's voice took on a weary quality. "Please choose efficient. I have seven more reports to file today."

Brentley looked at the collar. At the enforcement familiars. At Jarik, who stood frozen, unsure what to do. At Greeb, who looked simultaneously exhausted and determined.

Then the cat reached into... somewhere. It was unclear where. Cats don't have pockets. But somehow Brentley produced a crumpled piece of paper.

"Actually," he said, smoothing it out with one paw, "I have documentation."

Greeb's ears flattened. "What kind of documentation?"

"A Certificate of Emotional Independence." Brentley held up the paper. It was wrinkled, slightly singed, and covered in illegible scrawling. "Signed by God. Completely legitimate."

Silence.

"That's not a real thing," Greeb said.

"Prove it."

"The signature says 'God, probably.'"

"God is uncertain. It's theologically sound." Brentley's tail curled. "Also, there's a seal. See? A completely authentic seal."

"That's a paw print in what looks like jam."

"Celestial jam. Different thing."

The owl and rabbit exchanged glances. Greeb pinched the bridge of his nose with one paw—a gesture that looked strange on a corgi but conveyed perfect exasperation.

"Brentley," he said slowly. "That document is clearly forged."

"Is it? Have you verified it with God?"

"I—" Greeb stopped. "We don't have God on file."

"Exactly. So you can't prove it's forged." The cat looked smug. "Burden of proof. That's fundamental to legal proceedings."

"This isn't a legal proceeding. This is a recapture operation."

"Sounds like a legal proceeding to me." Brentley turned to Jarik. "Does this sound like a legal proceeding to you?"

"Don't bring me into this!"

"Too late. You're already documented as an accessory." The cat turned back to Greeb. "I invoke my right to proper documentation review. Regulation 27-F. All submitted paperwork must be verified before containment can proceed."

Greeb's left eye twitched—a tic he'd developed three months ago, around the time a certain cat had escaped his facility. "That regulation is for processing new familiars, not recapturing escaped ones."

"Does it specify that?"

"It's implied!"

"Implication isn't regulation." Brentley's purr rumbled. "You taught me that. Section 3, paragraph 8: 'All rules must be explicitly stated to be enforceable.' Your words. Your training."

The corgi stared at him. The owl shifted uncomfortably. The rabbit's stunner hummed with frustrated energy.

"You—" Greeb's eye twitched again. Brentley watched it with interest. "—are the most difficult familiar I have ever encountered."

"Thank you. Also, your eye is doing that thing," the cat observed.

"I'M AWARE... and that wasn't a compliment."

"I'm taking it as one."

Greeb opened his mouth to respond. A new alarm started blaring—different from the proximity alerts, higher pitched, more urgent.

Val's voice crackled through the speakers. "Warning. Power surge detected in secondary systems. Fire in the galley wiring."

Everyone froze.

"The what?" Greeb said.

"Coffee machine," Jarik said weakly. "The fire from the console—it must have spread through the wiring—"

He looked at Brentley. At the spilled coffee from hours ago. At the sparks that had seemed harmless.

"Oh no," he said.

"Oh yes," Brentley purred.

And the coffee machine exploded.

CHAPTER 7

CONTAINMENT PROTOCOL

The explosion wasn't large. In the grand scheme of cosmic disasters, it barely registered. But in the confined space of the *Marginal Profit*'s galley, it was more than sufficient.

The coffee machine—already damaged, already smoking, already held together by spite and poor maintenance—detonated in a shower of sparks, scalding liquid, and what might have been ectoplasm. The blast knocked Greeb sideways. The owl shrieked, flapped instinctively, and slammed into the ceiling. The rabbit's stunner discharged into a wall panel.

And Brentley, sitting on the console, didn't look surprised at all.

"Told you it was broken," he said.

Jarik dove for the fire suppression controls. "Val! Emergency protocols!"

"Activating suppression systems. Also, I should mention —the coffee machine explosion has compromised the gravity stabilizers."

"What does that mean?"

"It means," Val said apologetically, "in approximately ten seconds, we're going to experience significant gravitational fluctuations."

Greeb scrambled to his feet, fur singed. "What did you DO?"

"Me?" Brentley examined his claws. "Nothing. The coffee machine's been unstable since before I arrived. Ask the captain."

Jarik's hand hovered over the fire suppression override. The system was already activating—foam dispensers priming, ready to spray. But there, on the panel, was the manual control. Full discharge. Immediate.

They're going to take Brentley. They're going to impound my ship.

The old cargo-run tension settled between his shoulder blades.

Unless they can't see.

"The fire wouldn't have spread if you hadn't spilled coffee everywhere!" he said, buying himself a heartbeat to think.

"I didn't spill the coffee. You did. When you hit me with your ship. Also, you might want to hold onto something."

"Why?"

Jarik slammed his palm down on the manual override.

Every suppression nozzle in the ship activated simultaneously. Not the controlled spray designed for targeted fires—the emergency flood meant for catastrophic breaches. White foam exploded from the ceiling, the walls, the floor panels. It filled the cabin in seconds, a blinding cloud of chemical suppressant.

The gravity cut out.

Jarik's stomach lurched as his feet left the deck. The foam became a churning storm of white globules, filling every cubic meter of space. He couldn't see two feet in front of him. Could barely breathe through the chemical smell.

He grabbed for where he remembered the handhold being. Found it. Held on.

Around him, chaos erupted in white.

"I can't see!" Greeb's voice, muffled and furious, somewhere to the left. "Where's the familiar?"

The owl shrieked. Wings flapping frantically, creating currents in the foam. The rabbit's squeak came out three octaves higher than regulation allowed: "Sir! The foam! I can't—"

"This violates safety regulations!" Greeb shouted.

Jarik pulled himself along the handhold, blind in the chemical fog. *Did that just work? Did I just—*

"Val," he gasped. "Where's Brentley?"

"Forward console. Hasn't moved. Remarkably calm, considering."

Of course he was.

Through the white blur, Jarik could just make out movement. The owl's wings creating vortexes in the foam. The rabbit tumbling past, ears streaming bubbles. Greeb's silhouette, paddling desperately, his clipboard spinning away like a tiny UFO.

Brentley's voice cut through the chaos, perfectly composed. "Quantum declawed. I mentioned that."

The foam slowly began to dissipate, pulled toward the air recyclers. Visibility returned in patches. Jarik could see Greeb floating upside down, his legs paddling at nothing, covered head to tail in white foam. The owl had somehow gotten tangled in its own armor straps. The rabbit hung from a cable at an awkward angle, its weapon pointing at its own feet.

Brentley sat on the wall—attached somehow, claws gripping metal that shouldn't be grippable—looking entirely too pleased with himself.

And not looking at Jarik.

But his tail twitched once. A small gesture. *Well done.*

Greeb finally oriented himself, foam dripping from his fur. His eyes locked on Jarik. "Did you just—"

"Emergency fire response," Jarik said quickly. His heart hammered. "Standard protocol for electrical fires in confined spaces."

"That was NOT standard—"

"Val," Jarik interrupted. "How long until gravity's back?"

"Unknown. The stabilizers are trying to compensate, but the coffee machine's power surge created a feedback loop. Could be thirty seconds. Could be thirty minutes."

"Thirty minutes?"

"Or it could be permanent. The diagnostic protocols are unstable right now."

Greeb used his short legs to push off a wall, launching himself toward his floating clipboard. "This is unacceptable! We're trying to conduct an official operation!"

"Should have done it before the coffee machine exploded," Brentley observed.

"The coffee machine shouldn't have exploded!"

"And yet." The cat's tail lashed, the motion sending him drifting along the wall. "Funny how things that shouldn't happen keep happening around me."

The corgi's eyes narrowed. He twisted in midair, orienting himself toward Brentley. "You planned this."

"I planned for a coffee machine I'd never seen before to explode at exactly the right moment? I'm good, but I'm not that good."

"You caused the spill that started the fire!"

"Did I? I was the one floating in space, minding my own business, when someone hit me with a ship." The cat examined his claws. "Can't be held responsible for every mechanical failure that happens after someone commits vehicular cat-slaughter."

"Vehicular—you're not dead!"

"Well, yes. I'm very hard to kill. But the principle stands."

Greeb opened his mouth to respond when the rabbit's stunner went off again. The bolt of energy shot across the cabin, missed everyone, and hit a control panel. The lights flickered. An alarm started blaring. And somewhere in the walls, something began making a grinding noise.

"Sorry!" the rabbit squeaked. "It's the zero-G! My trigger discipline isn't calibrated for—"

"Just put the stunner away!" Greeb commanded, spinning to face his subordinate.

"I'm trying! My holster is oriented for gravity!"

The owl swooped past, trying to help. Its talons caught on the rabbit's armor. Both familiars went tumbling across the cabin in a tangle of feathers and fur.

Brentley watched this with what might have been amusement. "Your enforcement team needs training."

"They're excellent in normal gravity!" Greeb snapped, paddling through the air toward the struggling pair. "This is an unusual circumstance!"

"Unusual circumstances are basically my whole thing."

The cat pushed off the wall, floating toward the console where Jarik still clung. "You should have prepared for unusual circumstances."

"I prepared for seventeen different scenarios!" Greeb grabbed the owl's wing, trying to separate it from the rabbit. "Ambush. Flight. Resistance. Hostage situations. Seventeen scenarios!"

"But not coffee machines?"

"Why would I prepare for a COFFEE MACHINE?"

"Lack of imagination." Brentley settled on the console next to Jarik, somehow gripping it despite the zero-G. "That's always been the Bureau's weakness. You plan for everything you can imagine, but never for what you can't."

Greeb finally pulled the owl and rabbit apart. Both familiars looked disheveled and embarrassed. The corgi pointed at them firmly. "Stay. There. Don't move."

They tried to stay still. The owl's instinct to flap made this difficult. The rabbit's ears kept floating upward, dragging it toward the ceiling.

Greeb turned back to Brentley, paddling through the air. He'd somehow kept hold of his clipboard through all of this, which was impressive or concerning.

"You think you're clever," he said.

"I know I'm clever." Brentley sounded entirely unbothered. "The question is whether you're clever enough to catch me."

"I caught you once."

"Did you?" The cat's eyes gleamed. "Or did I let myself be caught so I could study your procedures from the inside?"

The corgi's eye started up again—that rhythmic twitch

that seemed to activate whenever Brentley spoke. "You're claiming the first capture was intentional?"

"I'm claiming nothing. I'm simply suggesting that perhaps my presence in your facility was exactly where I wanted to be. For exactly as long as I wanted to be there." Brentley let the question linger. "How else would I have learned all your regulations well enough to cite them back at you?"

There was a pause. Greeb floated there, clipboard clutched in his paws, thinking this through.

"That's... actually concerning."

"You'd think so." Brentley purred.

"But also probably a lie."

"Probably."

"You're just making things up to buy time."

"Am I?" The cat examined his claws. "Or am I revealing a long-term plan that you're only now beginning to understand?"

Jarik, still clinging to his handhold, finally spoke up. "Can we maybe focus on the immediate problem? Like the gravity? Or the alarms? Or the fact that my ship is attached to yours and both are currently malfunctioning?"

Greeb turned to him, and for a moment, Jarik thought he saw suspicion in those dark eyes. But then the corgi shook his head, foam flying. "You. The captain. How long until your ship is functional?"

"How would I know? I'm not an engineer! I just fly the thing!" Jarik gestured helplessly at the console. "Val, status update?"

"Systems are experiencing cascading failures," Val

reported. "The good news is nothing else has exploded. The bad news is everything else is thinking about exploding."

"That's not encouraging!"

"I'm not programmed for encouragement. I'm programmed for accurate status reports." Val paused. "We're doomed. Probably."

"Was that last part necessary?"

"Statistically accurate."

Greeb paddled closer to the console, trying to assess the damage himself. "We need to get gravity back online. I can't conduct a proper containment procedure in these conditions."

"Have you tried asking nicely?" Brentley suggested.

"Asking what nicely?"

"Gravity. Maybe it needs positive reinforcement."

The corgi's eye twitched. He turned to his enforcement team. "Status report. What's your assessment?"

The owl, still trying to stay stationary, spoke in a clipped tone. "Sir, recommend we abort containment and retreat to the *Perpetual Compliance*. Conduct operation from controlled environment."

"Seconded," the rabbit squeaked. "This vessel is compromised."

Greeb looked torn. Retreating made tactical sense. But it meant admitting defeat—even temporarily.

Brentley watched this internal struggle with interest. "It's okay to retreat, you know. It's quite strategic. God would approve."

"I don't take advice from escaped familiars."

"Your loss. I have excellent strategic insights." The cat's tail flicked. "For instance, I can tell you that in approximately fifteen seconds, the backup power is going to fail."

Everyone froze.

"How do you know that?" Jarik asked.

"The smell. Burning circuitry has an unmistakable odor. Also, that panel is sparking." Brentley pointed with one paw at a wall panel that was indeed throwing small sparks into the zero-G environment. "Fifteen seconds. Maybe twelve."

Greeb's ears flattened. "Everyone back to the ship! Now!"

The owl didn't need to be told twice. It spread its wings and swooped toward the airlock. The rabbit followed, using its powerful legs to launch itself in the right direction. Greeb grabbed his clipboard and paddled after them.

Then he stopped.

Turned back to look at Brentley.

"This isn't over," he said.

"Of course not," Brentley replied. "You haven't filled out the forms yet."

"I'm going to get you back in custody. Properly. With documentation." The corgi's voice was firm. "And when I do, I'm adding 'obstruction of justice' to your file."

"Looking forward to it." The cat's eyes gleamed. "Though you might want to hurry. Ten seconds now."

Greeb swore—a remarkably dignified, bureaucratic swear—and launched himself toward the airlock.

He almost made it.

Then the backup power failed.

The lights cut out completely. Emergency systems kicked in, bathing everything in red. The alarms changed pitch, becoming more urgent. And somewhere deep in the ship, something important stopped working with a sound like a mechanical death rattle.

"Val?" Jarik called into the darkness.

"Still here. Barely. Running on emergency reserves." Val's voice crackled. "The good news is the gravity should be back soon."

"How soon?"

"Five seconds."

"That's not enough time to—"

Gravity returned.

Everyone fell.

Greeb hit the deck with a thud and an undignified yelp. The owl crashed into a bulkhead. The rabbit landed on its face. Jarik, still holding his handhold, merely dropped a few inches.

And Brentley, somehow, landed perfectly on all four paws on the console.

"See?" he said. "Cats always land on their feet. It's not physics. It's philosophy."

Greeb pushed himself up, fur disheveled, dignity compromised. His clipboard had landed several feet away, its magical glow flickering. The corgi limped toward it, picked it up, and turned to glare at Brentley.

"I'm adding 'making me fall' to the charges."

"That's not a regulation."

"I'll make it one." Greeb helped his enforcement team up. The owl looked dazed. The rabbit was muttering something about proper landing procedures. "You okay?"

"Operational," the owl said.

"Bruised," the rabbit squeaked.

"Good enough." Greeb turned back to Brentley. His eyes

narrowed. "Last chance. Come quietly, or we do this the difficult way."

"I choose difficult. It's more interesting."

"That's what I thought." The corgi nodded to the owl. "Get the collar."

The owl produced the containment collar again—still glowing, still inscribed with those uncomfortable symbols. It moved toward Brentley cautiously, talons ready to grab if the cat bolted.

Brentley watched it approach, apparently unconcerned.

"You know," he said conversationally, "I should mention I have a medical exemption for neck accessories."

"You don't," Greeb said, consulting his clipboard. "We've been over this."

"No, really. I have a documented sensitivity to magical restraints." The cat's whiskers twitched. "It's genetic and very rare. It causes spontaneous reality fluctuations."

"That's not in your file."

"You sure?" Brentley's eyes gleamed. "Check section 7. Subsection 12. Medical notes."

Greeb flipped through his clipboard. Found the section. Squinted at it. "This just says 'Subject claims everything. Verify nothing.'"

"See? Verify nothing. That's an instruction. You haven't verified that I don't have a medical exemption."

"That's not how medical exemptions work!"

"Are you sure?"

The owl reached for Brentley. The cat didn't move, just watched with those too-intelligent eyes. The collar came closer. Closer. Almost touching fur—

Brentley coughed.

Everyone froze.

"Oh no," Brentley said.

"What 'oh no'?" Greeb demanded. "What does 'oh no' mean?"

The cat's throat worked. His shoulders hunched. His tail went rigid.

"Don't," Jarik said, recognizing the signs. "Don't you dare—"

Brentley coughed again. Harder.

And produced a hairball.

But not a normal hairball. This hairball glowed. Pulsed. It radiated colors that shouldn't exist—ultraviolet purple mixed with infrared green, quantum blue swirled with probability orange. It sat on the deck plating, roughly the size of a marble, and hummed with energy that made Jarik's teeth ache.

Silence.

Everyone stared at it.

"Well," Brentley said, looking at his creation with mild interest. "That was inconvenient."

Greeb's voice came out dangerously quiet. "Brentley. What is that?"

"A hairball." Brentley licked a paw. "I groom regularly. These things happen."

"That—" the corgi pointed at the glowing, pulsing, reality-warping object on the deck, "—is not a normal hairball."

"I'm not a normal cat."

The owl backed away slowly. The rabbit's ears had gone completely flat. Even Jarik was edging toward the far wall.

Greeb pulled a scanner from his vest. Pointed it at the

hairball. The scanner immediately began screaming—not metaphorically, but actually producing a high-pitched shriek of electronic distress.

"That's a Class-7 Reality Residue," Greeb said, his voice climbing an octave. "You coughed up a Class-7 Reality Residue!"

"Did I?" Brentley examined the hairball with professional interest. "How about that."

"HOW ABOUT THAT?" The corgi's professional composure was cracking. "Do you know what Class-7 residues can do?"

"Explode?"

"WORSE THAN EXPLODE!"

The hairball pulsed brighter.

"NOBODY MOVE," Greeb commanded.

No one was moving. Even Brentley had gone still, tail rigid, watching his hairball with renewed attention.

"Okay," Jarik said carefully. "So. What do we do?"

"We don't touch it. We don't look at it too hard. And we definitely don't let it get near any power sources or dimensional interfaces." Greeb's eyes were locked on the hairball. "Owl, get the containment foam. Rabbit, prepare suppression protocols. We need to stabilize it before—"

The hairball rolled.

Just slightly. A tiny movement, like it was testing the deck.

"DON'T MOVE!" Greeb shouted again.

Jarik froze. But his foot—already shifting his weight when the order came—completed its motion. His boot came down on a piece of debris. A fragment of the rabbit's equipment harness, knocked loose during the zero-G chaos.

It skittered across the deck.

Struck the hairball.

The glowing orb rolled. Picked up speed. Headed directly toward the airlock.

Toward the docking tube and the *Perpetual Compliance*.

"NO!" Greeb lunged.

The owl dove. Missed. The rabbit scrambled forward. Also missed. The hairball rolled past them, faster now, as if it had been waiting for exactly this nudge.

Jarik stood frozen, his boot still where it had landed. *I just—I didn't—*

Brentley's eyes met his for just a heartbeat. And in them, Jarik saw something that might have been approval. Or might have been shared horror at what they'd just set in motion.

"That's new," the cat said quietly.

"New?" Jarik's voice came out strangled.

"Usually they just sit there." Brentley's tail twitched. "This one has initiative."

The hairball reached the airlock and rolled through. It entered the docking tube connecting the two ships.

Greeb's ears flattened completely. "It's heading for my ship."

"Technically the Bureau's ship," Brentley corrected.

"NOT HELPFUL!"

Everyone ran—or flew, or hopped—toward the airlock. Through the open docking tube, they could see the hairball rolling along, leaving a trail of sparkles that smelled like burning circuitry and something else. Something that made the air taste wrong.

It reached the *Perpetual Compliance*'s airlock.

Rolled through.

And disappeared into the pristine white corridors of the Bureau vessel.

"Where's it going?" Jarik asked, though he already knew he didn't want the answer.

Greeb's voice was hollow. "Engineering. They always go to engineering."

"How do you know?"

"Because that's where the hyperdrive is." The corgi stared. "And Reality Residues are attracted to dimensional technology."

They watched as distant lights flickered on the Bureau ship. An alarm started blaring. Figures moved in the corridors—crew members scrambling, trying to contain whatever was happening.

"Can they stop it?" Brentley asked, genuinely curious.

"They can try." Greeb's ears had flattened completely. "But a Class-7 coming into contact with an active hyperdrive..."

He didn't finish the sentence. He didn't need to.

Deep in the *Perpetual Compliance*, something began to glow.

Jarik's hands gripped the edge of the airlock. He couldn't look away. Couldn't process. A hairball. A *hairball*. Rolling toward a hyperdrive like it had purpose, like it knew—

And then, beautifully, catastrophically, inevitably—

For half a second the ship was both there and not there, the universe negotiating which version of the next moment to keep.

Then it decided.

The Bureau ship imploded.

Not exploded. Imploded. The entire vessel collapsed in on itself like a star dying in reverse, shrinking down to a point of impossible light before bursting outward in a shower of glittering particles that caught the nebula's glow. The laws of physics, Jarik's mind supplied helpfully, *don't allow that.* Ships don't implode. Matter doesn't just vanish into points of light. Hyperdrives catastrophically failing produce explosions, not—not *whatever that was.*

But he'd seen it. Watched it happen. The pristine white hull folding in on itself like paper, the gold trim stretching and snapping, the crew inside—

Oh god, the crew.

"Get back!" someone shouted—maybe him, maybe Greeb. They scrambled away from the docking tube as the shockwave hit. The connection shuddered. Alarms shrieked. Emergency bulkheads began sliding shut—too slow, always too slow—

The *Marginal Profit* lurched as the docking clamps disengaged automatically. The tube separated. And through the forward viewport, they watched the glittering dust slowly disperse into the nebula, along with a few spinning pieces of debris.

A clipboard tumbled past the viewport, its magical glow fading. A filing cabinet, spilling forms that disintegrated in the vacuum.

And then—lights. Dozens of them. Escape pods tumbling away from where the ship had been, emergency beacons blinking in the darkness. The crew had gotten out. Somehow.

Jarik's hands wouldn't stop shaking. He stared at the space where a ship had been—a massive, Leviathan-class enforcement frigate with crew quarters and a cafeteria and state-of-the-art systems that someone had spent six months building—

"I did that," he heard himself say. "I kicked—the hairball rolled because I—"

"You didn't do anything." Brentley's voice, surprisingly gentle. "I did." Jarik turned to stare at him. The cat sat on the console, looking at the viewport with something that might have been regret. Or might have been satisfaction. It was impossible to tell.

"That was the Bureau's newest enforcement vessel," Greeb said. His voice came from far away. He floated in the middle of the cabin, still gripping his clipboard, staring at nothing. "Six months of construction. State-of-the-art systems. *Gone.*"

The universe, Jarik thought distantly, had rules. Physics. Logic. Things you could count on. Gravity pulled down. Vacuum killed you. Ships didn't just *stop existing*. But he'd just watched it happen. The rules were suggestions. Reality was negotiable. And he'd just helped a cat destroy a government vessel with a hairball.

What is my life?

Brentley broke the silence.

"Well," he said. "That was inconvenient."

CHAPTER 8

THE HAIRBALL INCIDENT

Nobody moved.

The glittering debris that had been the *Perpetual Compliance* drifted past the viewport, catching the nebula's light. A clipboard spun by, its magical glow fading. What might have been a filing cabinet tumbled through space, spilling forms that immediately disintegrated.

Greeb stared at the destruction. His clipboard hung forgotten in one paw. His other paw made small, helpless gestures at the viewport, like he was trying to calculate the paperwork for this and coming up with numbers his brain refused to process.

"That was the Bureau's newest enforcement vessel." Greeb's voice was hollow.

"Was being the operative word," Brentley observed.

"Six months of construction. State-of-the-art systems. Magical shielding rated for Class-9 reality breaches." His voice remained flat, mechanical. "Gone. Because of a hairball."

"Not just any hairball." The cat examined his claws. "A special hairball. With initiative."

The owl had gone completely still, staring at the debris field. The rabbit had its paws over its eyes, muttering something about early retirement and farming.

Jarik found his voice first. "How? How does a hairball—how does ANY hairball—do that?"

"Reality Residue," Greeb said mechanically, still staring at the viewport. "Accumulates in beings who've been exposed to too much dimensional energy. Temporal rifts. Probability storms. Quantum paradoxes." He turned slowly to look at Brentley. "Where have you BEEN?"

"I took a nap near the Oort Cloud Anomaly. Spent a weekend in a temporal eddy off Rigel VII. You know, the usual tourist traps."

"That's not a normal travel itinerary!"

"I'm not a normal cat." The cat hopped down from the console. "Though I am surprised about the whole implosion thing. Usually my hairballs just smell bad."

"USUALLY?"

"I don't cough them up often. Maybe once every few decades." Brentley padded toward the viewport, examining the debris with professional interest. "This one was particularly energetic. Must have absorbed more than I thought."

Greeb's eye twitched. "You've done this before."

"Not the destroying-a-ship part. That's new. Though there was an incident with a filing cabinet once. It was unfortunate. There was paperwork everywhere."

"I'm going to be demoted." Greeb's voice went hollow. His ears drooped completely, hanging limp against his head. "They're going to demote me so hard I'll be back to guarding supply closets."

"Look on the bright side," Brentley offered. "You survived. Your team survived. No casualties."

"MY SHIP IS GONE!"

"Details."

The rabbit lowered its paws. "Sir? What are our orders?"

Greeb stared at it. At the owl. At the destroyed ship. At Brentley, who looked entirely too pleased with himself. The corgi's shoulders slumped. He set his clipboard down on a nearby surface with a sigh that seemed to come from his soul.

"Orders," he said. "Right. Orders." He looked at the clipboard like it had personally betrayed him, then at the viewport where his ship used to be. "I should... file a report. Requisition a new vessel. Document the loss. Calculate damages."

"Sounds tedious," Brentley said.

"It's my JOB!" Greeb's professional composure was fracturing. "Everything I do is tedious! That's what the Bureau IS! Tedious documentation of magical anomalies! And YOU—" he pointed at Brentley with a shaking paw, "—are the MOST tedious anomaly I have ever encountered!"

"Is that my official designation now? I prefer it to 7734. It has more personality."

Greeb took a breath. Then another. Trying to regain control. When he spoke again, his voice was forced-calm. "Brentley. You have just destroyed Bureau property worth approximately four hundred thousand credits. The paperwork alone—months. Years, possibly."

"I didn't destroy anything. My hairball did." The cat sat down, wrapping his tail around his paws. "I can't be held responsible for my autonomous bodily functions."

"That hairball came from YOU!"

"Did it? Can you prove ownership? I certainly didn't sign anything claiming it." Brentley's eyes gleamed. "Sounds like a legal gray area to me."

The corgi's other eye started twitching to match the first.

Jarik, watching this exchange, finally found enough courage to speak. "So. What happens now?"

Everyone turned to look at him.

"What happens," Greeb's paw trembled as he picked up his clipboard again, "is that I'm going to arrest all of you. Transport you to Bureau headquarters. In a different ship. Which I will have to requisition. Which will take weeks." His voice was climbing again. "Weeks of waiting while sitting in this malfunctioning cargo hauler with a reality-warping cat and an accessory to familiar harboring!"

"Or," Brentley suggested, "you could let us go."

Greeb's eye had gone still for the first time since boarding. He was actually considering it.

"Let you go," Greeb repeated.

"Yes. It's simple. Clean. There wouldn't be any additional paperwork. You go back to headquarters and report that I was destroyed in the implosion. It was a tragic accident. Case closed."

"You're not destroyed."

"Are you sure? Did you scan for survivors?" Brentley gestured at the debris field. "Lots of glittering particles out there. Any of those could be me. Quantum mechanics are uncertain."

"I'm looking directly at you."

"Are you though? How do you know I'm not a probability echo? Or a temporal afterimage? Reality is extremely fluid around hairball incidents." The cat's eyes gleamed. "Check your scanner. I bet my signature is highly unclear right now."

Despite himself, Greeb pulled out his scanner. Pointed it

at Brentley. The device made a confused noise, displayed several contradictory readings, then gave up and showed a question mark.

"See?" Brentley said. "Highly uncertain. I could be here. I could be not here. Schrodinger would be proud."

"That's not how any of this works!"

"That's one perspective." The cat tilted his head. "You're the Bureau. You love technicalities. 'Subject's quantum signature indeterminate following Class-7 Reality Residue event.' File it under 'presumed neutralized' and move on."

Greeb stared at him. At the scanner. At his clipboard. At the destroyed ship.

Jarik's mouth moved before he fully realized what he was doing. "Think about the alternative."

Everyone turned to look at him.

"Think about it," he continued, his voice gaining strength. "I've hauled freight through three sectors. I know logistics. I know bureaucracy." He gestured at the debris field. "That was a Leviathan-class enforcement frigate. Do you know what investigating its loss involves?"

Greeb's ears twitched.

"Environmental impact reports for the nebula contamination," Jarik counted off on his fingers. "Depositions from every crew member's family. Hearings with the Bureau's oversight committee—assuming they have one. Forensic analysis of debris scattered across half a sector. Insurance claims. Multiple jurisdictions arguing over responsibility." He looked Greeb dead in the eye. "It'll take *years*."

The corgi's paw loosened on his clipboard.

"Or," Jarik said quietly, "you file one report. 'Class-

Omega familiar presumed neutralized in catastrophic reality breach. No recoverable evidence. Case closed.' One report. Done. You go home."

The owl spoke up quietly. "Sir, he has a point. Procedurally speaking."

"Don't help him!"

"I'm just saying, if the readings are indeterminate, we can't definitively prove—"

"I KNOW WHAT YOU'RE SAYING!" Greeb rounded on his enforcement team. "Are you suggesting we let the most wanted familiar in three sectors just... walk away?"

The rabbit raised a paw hesitantly. "Would it help if I said the alternative involves months of paperwork and possibly courts-martial for losing the newest enforcement vessel?"

The clipboard creaked in his paws. Nobody spoke.

Then, quietly, Greeb said: "How much paperwork?"

"Form 9-B for ship loss. Form 15-D for mission failure. Form 22-A for reality breach documentation. Form—"

"Stop." Greeb held up a paw. "Just... stop." He looked at Brentley. At Jarik. At his own defeated reflection in the viewport. "If I let you go—and I'm not saying I will—what's to stop you from causing more incidents?"

"Nothing," Brentley said cheerfully. "But I'll cause them far away from you. I'll be in different sectors and different jurisdictions. I wouldn't be your problem."

"That's not reassuring."

"It's honest though." The cat's tail swished. "And truthfully, don't you want to never see me again? Think about it. No more chasing me. No more hairballs. No more forms with my designation on them. Just... peace. And other people's problems."

Greeb looked like he was genuinely considering this. The owl and rabbit exchanged glances that said they were strongly in favor of this plan.

"There will be an investigation," Greeb said slowly. "About the ship. About what happened here."

"And you'll file a report," Brentley said. "It will be thoroughly detailed and accurate. Subject escaped during a reality breach event. Quantum signature was indeterminate. Threat presumed neutralized. You followed all protocols. There is nothing you could have done differently."

"They won't believe it."

"They won't want to pay for a new investigation. Budget constraints. Bureaucratic efficiency. Sometimes it's easier to close a case than it is to keep it open."

The corgi's grip on his clipboard loosened slightly. He looked at his team. "Thoughts?"

"I think," the owl said carefully, "that pursuing this further would be... resource-intensive."

"I think," the rabbit squeaked, "that I'd like to go home and never think about hairballs again."

Greeb turned back to Brentley. To Jarik. His expression was exhausted, defeated, and slightly relieved.

Three months. Two thousand four hundred and seventy-three forms. A clipboard that had cracked in a hairball-related incident two weeks ago and had to be returned to Procurement with a written justification for replacement. A career that until this morning had been on a smooth upward trajectory toward a senior position at a desk that did not move and a window that did not look out at any nebulae.

Filing this report meant filing the form he had spent three months trying not to file: the one with the box that said *Subject neutralized—outcome indeterminate*. It meant the smooth trajectory bent. It meant a demotion. It meant Director Archimor reading the file and saying something that Protocol 19-G would translate into an approval, but that everyone in the office would know was not, in the way that owls do not need to make their disappointment loud.

He looked at the cat. The cat looked back at him with the serene confidence of a creature who knew exactly what he was asking the corgi to give up, and was asking anyway.

"If I do this," he said, "if I file this report—you disappear. Completely. I never see you again. No incidents. No property damage. No more hairballs."

"Deal," Brentley said immediately.

"I'm serious. If I find out you're still causing problems—"

"You won't. Because you won't be looking." The cat hopped back onto the console. "Different sectors, remember? Not your jurisdiction. Not your problem."

Jarik finally found his voice. "Wait, are we actually being let go? After destroying a ship?"

"Allegedly neutralized during reality breach," Greeb corrected. "Entirely different from 'let go.'" He pointed at Jarik with his clipboard. "You were a victim of circumstance. Wrong place, wrong time. We're releasing you with a warning."

"A warning about what?"

"Don't pick up hitchhikers." Greeb's voice was flat. "Especially if they're in space. And especially if they're cats."

"That's very specific advice."

"You'd be surprised how often it comes up." The corgi's expression hardened. He stepped closer to Jarik, his voice dropping. "And Captain Venn? If you are ever seen with him again—in any sector, any station, any coordinates whatsoever—there will be no forms. There will be no discussion. There will be no warnings. Do you understand me?"

Jarik understood. This wasn't mercy. It was a calculated risk that Greeb was taking, and if it backfired, the corgi would come for them with everything the Bureau had.

"Understood," Jarik said quietly.

"Good." Greeb turned to his team. "We're leaving. Back to headquarters. To file many, many reports." He paused at the airlock, looking back at Brentley one final time. "I hope I never see you again."

"Likewise. Though you'll miss me. They always do. Give it a month—you'll be telling stories about me at Bureau social functions."

"We don't have social functions."

"That explains so much about your organization."

Greeb made a sound that might have been a growl or might have been resignation. He gestured to his team. The owl and rabbit followed him through the airlock, back into the docking tube, back toward... nothing. Their ship was gone.

"Wait," Jarik called out. "How are you getting back? Your ship is—"

"Emergency beacon," Greeb said without turning around. "Rescue protocols. Someone will come. Eventually." He paused in the airlock. "This conversation never happened. The cat is presumed neutralized. You were never involved. Understood?"

"Understood," Jarik said quickly.

"Good." The corgi looked at Brentley one last time. "If you are still alive—and I'm not officially acknowledging that you are—stay out of my jurisdiction."

"Define jurisdiction."

"EVERYWHERE I CAN FILE PAPERWORK!"

"Extremely specific. I'll try to remember that." Brentley's nose wrinkled. "Though my memory is highly uncertain. Quantum mechanics, you know."

Greeb's clipboard snapped in half.

The corgi looked at the broken pieces in his paws. At Brentley. Then back at the pieces. He dropped them, turned, and walked through the airlock without another word. The owl and rabbit hurried after him.

The inner airlock door hissed shut.

Jarik and Brentley stared at it.

"Did that just happen?" Jarik asked.

"Appears so." The cat settled more comfortably on the console. "Bureaucracy is a wonderful thing. Given enough paperwork, people will agree to almost anything to make it stop."

"You destroyed their ship."

"My autonomous bodily function destroyed their ship. I destroyed nothing." Brentley's eyes gleamed. "That's a very important legal distinction."

"That's insane."

"That's freedom." The cat started grooming a paw. "Also, you should probably undock before they change their minds."

Jarik blinked. Then lunged for the controls. "Val! Emergency undock!"

"Undocking," Val said. "Though I should mention, several systems are still confused about what just happened."

"Join the club." Jarik's hands flew across the console, disengaging the magnetic clamps. The *Marginal Profit* shuddered, pulling away from the docking tube. Through the viewport, he could see Greeb and his team floating in the tube, waiting for rescue that might take hours.

The corgi raised one paw. Not waving goodbye. Just... acknowledging. The gesture of one professional to another, united in their mutual exhaustion.

Jarik waved back.

Then the ship pulled free, engines firing, turning away from the debris field and the nebula and the bureaucratic nightmare they were leaving behind.

"Where to?" Val asked.

Jarik slumped in his chair, suddenly exhausted. "Anywhere. Somewhere quiet. Somewhere without talking cats or reality-warping hairballs or space animal control."

"So not here, then," Brentley said.

"NOT HERE!"

The cat purred, settling into the captain's chair. "Fair enough. Though I should warn you—quiet is overrated. And wherever we go, trouble will probably follow."

"We? There is no 'we.' I'm dropping you off at the first space station that'll take you."

"Mm." Brentley's eyes half-closed. "We'll see."

Through the viewport, the nebula's crystallized dust glittered around them. Behind them, the debris of the *Perpetual Compliance* slowly dispersed. Ahead, open space and infinite possibilities.

Jarik looked at the cat in his chair. At his damaged ship.

At his life, which had been simple and boring and safe exactly three hours ago.

"I should have left you on the windshield," he said.

Brentley's purr deepened.

"But you didn't."

And somehow, despite everything, it felt less like an ending than a start.

CHAPTER 9

EXIT STRATEGY

The *Marginal Profit* limped through space. Warning lights painted the cockpit in shades of red and amber. Something in the engine compartment made rhythmic clanging sounds. And there was smoke—not a lot of smoke, but enough to notice.

Jarik ignored it all. His hands gripped the controls, knuckles white, focusing on putting distance between them and the debris field. Between them and Greeb. Between them and every decision that had led to this moment.

"Status report," he said, voice hoarse.

Val's response crackled with static. "Hull integrity at seventy-three percent—the shockwave from the implosion didn't help. Life support's functional but complaining loudly. The engines are at sixty percent and considering early retirement. Coffee machine is—"

"Don't."

"—no longer a concern."

"Good." Jarik checked the sensors. No pursuit. No Bureau signatures. Just empty space and the slowly dispersing nebula behind them. "How far until we can jump?"

"Calculating. Approximately four minutes at current

speed." Val paused. "Though I should mention, jumping in our current condition is inadvisable."

"Everything today has been inadvisable."

"Fair point."

Brentley, still occupying the space atop the console, had begun grooming himself. Methodically. Calmly. Like he hadn't just destroyed a government vessel with a weaponized hairball.

Jarik watched him for a moment, then said: "We just destroyed a government vessel."

"Correction." Brentley paused mid-lick. "I liberated it from dimensional constraints. Very different thing."

"It exploded!"

"Imploded. Also different." The cat returned to grooming. "And technically, it was the hairball that did it. I was merely the delivery mechanism."

"That's not—" Jarik stopped, dragged a hand down his face. "You know what? I don't care. I don't care about the semantics of ship destruction. I don't care about your quantum hairballs. I just want to get somewhere safe and pretend this never happened."

"Pretending is healthy. Though safety is overrated."

"Says the cat who's been running from space animal control for three months."

"Exactly. Look how exciting my life is." The cat stretched, claws extending. "Yours was incredibly boring before I arrived. You should thank me."

Jarik's laugh came out slightly unhinged. "Thank you? THANK YOU? My ship is damaged. I'm probably wanted in multiple sectors. And I'm harboring the most dangerous familiar in known space!"

"Most interesting familiar. Dangerous is such a loaded word."

"You coughed up a reality-warping hairball!"

"Once. I've only done that once." Brentley examined a paw. "That we know of."

"THAT WE KNOW OF?"

"Memory is uncertain. Time is fluid. These things happen." The cat looked up with those too-intelligent eyes. "Besides, you're not harboring me. I'm choosing to stay. Entirely different dynamic."

"You're not staying! I'm dropping you off at the first—"

"Three minutes to jump capability," Val announced.

Jarik swallowed his protest and turned back to the controls. Something sparked. The smoke thickened.

"This is fine," he muttered. "Everything is fine."

"Excellent attitude." Brentley hopped down from the chair, padding across the console. "Remarkably positive. The ship responds well to affirmations."

"The ship responds to maintenance, which it hasn't had in six months because maintenance costs money I don't have."

"Then it's good you picked me up. I'm extremely lucky. Probably." The cat sat down directly on the navigation display, blocking half the readouts. "Things tend to work out when I'm around."

"Your definition of 'work out' is extremely different from mine."

"Tomato, space tomato."

Jarik reached around the cat, trying to see the display. Brentley didn't move. Just sat there, tail wrapped around his paws, looking pleased with himself.

"Can you not sit there?"

"I can. But I won't."

"Why?"

"This spot is warm. I like warm spots." Brentley's purr rumbled through the console. "Also, you need to learn to work around obstacles. It builds character."

"I have plenty of character!"

"Do you though?" The cat tilted his head. "You were hauling freeze-dried rations through a nebula shortcut to save three days. That's not character. That's resignation."

Jarik opened his mouth to argue, then closed it. Because the cat was right.

His gaze drifted to the small shelf beside the viewport. There, wedged between a broken chrono and a fire extinguisher bracket, was a photo. Him and Kess, taken six years ago at the shipyard where he'd bought the *Marginal Profit*. Both of them smiling, arms around each other, believing they were about to start something great.

He'd kept it there as a reminder. Of why he was doing this. Why he endured the boring hauls and the broken systems and the mounting debt.

But looking at it now, after everything that had just happened, it felt... distant. Like looking at someone else's life. Someone who'd believed safety and stability mattered more than anything.

Someone who'd never met a talking cat in space.

"Two minutes," Val said.

The ship groaned. Another panel sparked. The smoke alarm finally decided this qualified as an emergency and began shrieking.

"Val, disable that alarm."

"Already tried. It's having an existential crisis about what constitutes an emergency."

"Everything is an emergency!"

"Exactly. So nothing is. The alarm is confused." Val paused. "I understand the feeling."

Jarik let his hands fall away from the controls. Flexed his fingers, working out the stiffness from gripping too hard for too long. His head tilted back against the worn headrest—the padding long since flattened by years of use, the fabric smooth from countless jumps just like this one.

Except not like this one. Nothing had ever been like this one.

Around him, his ship fell apart in slow motion. Behind him, a crime scene drifted through space. And on his navigation display, a cat purred.

Jarik's voice dropped. "What was that hairball? Really."

Brentley's purr paused. "Lunch. Probably."

"Lunch doesn't destroy starships."

"Normal lunch doesn't. Mine is special." The cat resumed grooming. "I eat unusual things. Probability particles. Temporal anomalies. Once, a small paradox. It was very crunchy."

"That's not food."

"Everything is food if you're hungry enough." Brentley's tail twitched. "Do you really want details? They're not appetizing."

"I want to know what I'm dealing with. What you are." Jarik looked up, meeting the cat's eyes. "Because that wasn't just a hairball. That was something else. Something that made a Bureau enforcement director decide it was easier to let you go than document what happened."

"Smart man, that Greeb."

"Exhausted man. There's a difference."

"Is there?" The cat's eyes gleamed. "Maybe exhaustion is just wisdom wearing a different face."

"That's not profound. That's just word salad."

"All profound statements sound like word salad to the unprepared." Brentley stood, stretched. "One minute until jump, by the way. You should probably focus on not crashing us into a star."

Jarik grabbed the controls, checking vectors. The jump coordinates looked good. The ship looked terrible. The cat looked smug.

"This is insane," he muttered.

"Most good adventures are." Brentley padded toward the viewport, watching the stars. "You were hauling freight. Boring routes. Safe deliveries. Going nowhere interesting."

"Safe pays the bills!"

"Does it though? Your ship is held together with optimism. Your coffee maker just exploded. And according to your own records—which I may have glanced at while you were unconscious—you've been behind on payments for eighteen months."

Jarik's hands froze on the controls. "You looked at my records?"

"I was bored. You were unconscious for three seconds after the gravity came back. I'm an exceptionally fast reader." The cat's tail swished. "Point is, safety wasn't working for you anyway. So why not try excitement?"

"Because excitement involves destroying government property!"

"Only sometimes. Other times it just involves mild

property damage and interesting conversation." Brentley turned from the viewport. "Besides, you needed this. Something to remember. Something to tell people about."

"I was planning to retire quietly and forget everything!"

"Boring." The cat hopped back onto the console. "Also impossible. The Bureau will file reports. Your ship's signature is in their database. You're part of this now whether you like it or not."

"Thirty seconds," Val announced.

Jarik adjusted course slightly, preparing for the jump. The engines whined in protest but obeyed.

"When we get somewhere safe," he said, "you're leaving."

"You said that already." Brentley curled up on the console, closing his eyes. "Repetition doesn't make it more true."

"It's not repetition. It's emphasis."

"If you say so." Brentley's eyes closed.

"Ten seconds," Val said.

Jarik took a breath. Let it out. His hands moved across the controls with practiced efficiency, even as his mind screamed that nothing about this situation was efficient or practiced or sane.

The jump drive engaged.

Space twisted.

The *Marginal Profit* lurched forward into that strange not-space between places, where physics took a coffee break and causality went out for lunch.

For a moment, everything was quiet. No alarms. No sparks. No smoke. Just the strange humming of the jump drive and the even stranger sound of a cat purring.

Then they emerged into a different sector with different stars. Different problems, probably, but at least they weren't the same problems.

Jarik leaned back in his seat, utterly spent. His hands shook slightly. His ship groaned. And on his console, Brentley purred.

"We made it," he said.

"Obviously." The cat's eyes remained closed. "I told you. I'm very lucky."

"We destroyed a ship. Fled from the Bureau. Jumped through space in a barely functional hauler."

"And survived. Focus on the positive." Brentley's tail swished lazily. "You're alive. I'm alive. The ship is alive-adjacent. That's a win."

"That's not what winning feels like."

"Then you've been winning wrong." The cat's purr deepened. "Winning is supposed to feel like you barely survived. Otherwise, where's the accomplishment?"

Jarik stared at him. At the cat who'd hit his windshield, told impossible stories, destroyed government property, and was now napping on his console like none of it mattered.

"You're insane," he said.

"Probably." Brentley's whiskers twitched. "But I'm *interesting* insane, not boring insane. Important distinction. Besides, you needed excitement. Your ship smells like regret."

"My ship smells like burnt plastic and broken dreams."

"Same thing." The cat stretched without opening his eyes. "But now it also smells like adventure. And possibility. And slightly less regret."

"It smells like smoke."

"That's the adventure." Brentley's purr rumbled through the console. "You're welcome."

Jarik wanted to argue. Wanted to list all the reasons this wasn't welcome, wasn't wanted, wasn't anything except a disaster he'd accidentally rescued from space.

But looking at the cat—calm, confident, completely unbothered by the chaos he'd caused—Jarik found he couldn't quite summon the energy.

"Passengers pay, by the way."

"I paid in entertainment and excitement."

"That's not legal tender!"

"Isn't it?" Brentley finally opened one eye. "You haven't smiled this much in years. I checked your face muscles. Very rusty. But improving."

"I haven't smiled at all!"

"You smiled when Greeb's clipboard broke. I saw it." The cat's eye closed again. "Very brief. But definite."

The denial died in his throat. He had smiled—just for a second, at the absurdity and the chaos and the sheer bureaucratic defeat in Greeb's expression.

He settled deeper into his chair, staring at the ceiling. The worn photo on the shelf caught his eye again. Kess's smile. His own younger face. All those plans that had slowly unraveled into debt and loneliness.

Maybe Brentley's right, he thought. *Maybe safety was just another word for slowly dying.*

"This is the worst day of my life," he said.

"So far," Brentley purred.

"That's not comforting."

"Wasn't meant to be. Comfort is overrated. Excitement is where it's at."

"I hate you."

"No you don't." The cat's purr deepened into something that might have been satisfaction or might have been laughter. "But you will. Probably. And then you'll get over it. That's how these things work."

Jarik closed his eyes. His ship hummed around him—damaged, smoking, barely functional, but flying. Behind them, a crime scene. Ahead of them, unknown space and uncertain futures.

And on his console, a cat purred. The sound filled the cabin, steady and certain and somehow reassuring despite everything.

The stars drifted past the viewport. The ship groaned. And somewhere in the distance, probably, the Bureau was filing paperwork.

But for now, in this moment, they were free.

Even if it didn't feel like it.

Even if it felt like the beginning of something much worse.

The cat purred on, and against his better judgment, Jarik felt himself start to relax.

Jarik opened his mouth to say it again—*you're leaving at the first station*—but the words felt hollow now. He'd already said it. Multiple times. The cat hadn't believed him once.

"You're going to say 'we'll see' again, aren't you?" he muttered.

"I was going to say 'obviously.' But yours works too." Brentley's tail swished. "Wake me when we get there. Or when something explodes. Whichever comes first."

Jarik stared at the cat. At the stars. At his life, which had gone from boring to catastrophic in the span of three hours.

"I should've left you on the windshield," he said.

Brentley's purr deepened, satisfied and smug and entirely too knowing.

"But you didn't."

Jarik sat in silence for a moment, then asked, "Class-Omega. What does that actually mean?"

Brentley didn't answer right away. Long enough that Jarik thought he might not at all.

"It means I've died," he said finally. "Eight times. And come back. Eight times."

Something in his voice had gone level. Not flat—*level*, the voice of someone who'd learned to say it without bleeding around the words.

Jarik's hands stilled on the controls. "You're on your last life."

"Yes."

"Like... actually? Nine lives, like the saying?"

"Like the reality." Brentley's tail swished. "I don't know why. I don't know how. But every time I die, I wake up somewhere else. Alive. With one less life to spend."

He said it like reading from a record he had read many times. "It is not gentle. It is not painless. It is not a clean rebirth on some warm sunlit afternoon. I am wherever I am when it happens—sometimes a freighter, sometimes a moon, sometimes a vacuum I would prefer not to discuss—and then I am elsewhere. With less. Always with less." His purr rumbled, low and unbothered as a fact of weather. "I've got one left."

"And you spent today destroying a Bureau ship."

"I spent today staying free." The cat's eyes gleamed. "If this is my last life, I'm living it on my terms. Not theirs."

The gleam faded. He looked, for half a second, very small. Very orange. Very far from the towering self-aggrandizing thing that had explained card-counting and bureaucratic loopholes and the philosophical implications of pants. Just a cat with one breath of nine left to draw, choosing where to draw it.

Then the mask went back on. "Also, the Bureau ship was rude."

Jarik looked at the cat. At the stars. At his own three-fingered hands, steady on the controls for the first time in hours.

He had not expected to be the kind of man who steered toward someone's last life. He had been, for six years, the kind of man who steered toward fuel and contracts and the next paying drop—never toward a stake, never toward a person, never toward a thing that could be lost.

One life left. And he's spending it with me.

He didn't know what to do with that.

CHAPTER 10

THE PURRFECT GETAWAY

Two hours later, the *Marginal Profit* drifted through empty space. The fire in the galley had gone out. Mostly. There were still small flames in one corner, but Jarik had stopped caring around the time the third emergency system failed. The ship was flying. That was enough.

He sat at the console, running diagnostics he didn't want to read. Every system reported damage. Some were honest about it. Others just displayed error messages that translated roughly to "I give up."

"Val," he said. "Give me the full report."

"Are you sure?"

"No. Do it anyway."

Val's voice carried a note of sympathy. "Hull integrity is at sixty-eight percent and falling slowly. Life support is functional but resentful. The coffee machine is a memory. Engines are operating on what I can only describe as spite and momentum. The jump drive needs three weeks of maintenance we can't afford. And—" Val paused, "—we appear to be wanted."

Jarik's head dropped into his hands. "Wanted."

"Nine sectors. Possibly ten—the database keeps updating. These appear to be pre-existing warrants from Brentley's original escape."

Jarik's voice came out muffled by his palms. "What about Greeb's report? He said he'd mark Brentley as—"

Brentley, who had been napping on the dashboard for the past hour, opened one eye. "Presumed neutralized. Yes. But he's still floating in a docking tube waiting for rescue. Could be hours before he reaches headquarters. Days before the paperwork processes." His tail swished. "The old warrants are still active until his report clears the system. Bureaucracy moves slowly."

The console flickered.

"Update," Val said slowly. "The warrant count has changed."

"Changed how?" Jarik asked.

"Seven sectors now. Not nine." Val sounded confused. "The database revised itself. Two entries simply... aren't there anymore."

Jarik stared at the display. Then at Brentley.

The cat decided to groom his paw with studied disinterest. "See? Told you. Bureaucracy moves slowly. Databases are unreliable. Space communication delays. Solar interference. Cosmic rays affecting storage crystals. Very common."

"That's not—" Jarik stopped. The number had dropped. He'd watched it drop. Right after Brentley said bureaucracy moves slowly, and suddenly—

No. That's insane.

He shook his head. "Seven sectors. Still bad."

"Could be worse," Brentley said. "Could be nine. And once Greeb's report files, it'll be zero. We just need to stay quiet until then."

The console display held steady at seven.

Jarik decided not to think about it too hard.

"Wait," he said. "Those warrants—are they for *me* or for *you*?"

"Me. Obviously. I'm the escaped familiar who destroyed a hangar door. You're just my registered transportation provider."

Jarik lifted his head. "That's not a thing."

"It is now. I filed the paperwork mentally."

"YOU CAN'T FILE PAPERWORK MENTALLY!"

"I just did. Remarkably efficient. No physical forms required." The cat stretched, claws extending. "You should feel honored. Few beings get designated as my official transportation."

"I didn't agree to this!"

"Didn't you? You picked me up. Brought me aboard. Fed me—"

"I didn't feed you anything!"

"You had snacks in that cabinet. Terribly stale. But adequate." Brentley's tail swished. "Point is, you facilitated my transportation across space. That's literally the definition of a transportation provider."

Jarik stared at him. "You ate my emergency rations?"

"Emergency implies immediate need. I needed them immediately. Therefore, emergency." The cat settled back down, curling into a tighter ball. "Your logic is delightfully circular. I approve."

"That's not—" Jarik stopped himself. Took a breath. Let it out slowly. "You know what? Fine. Eat whatever you want. Destroy whatever you want. File imaginary paperwork. I'm too tired to argue."

"Excellent. Acceptance is the first stage of—"

"Don't finish that sentence."

"—partnership. I was going to say partnership."

"We're not partners."

"Aren't we? You're flying. I'm providing navigational critique and existential commentary. That's a partnership."

"That's a hostage situation."

The cat yawned, showing far too many teeth. "Wake me when something interesting happens."

Jarik turned back to the console, trying to focus on the damage reports. Behind him, small flames still flickered in the galley. The ship made concerning noises. And on his dashboard, a cat purred.

For a moment—just a brief, strange moment—it almost felt peaceful.

The stars outside were brilliant. No nebula to interfere. No Bureau ships in pursuit. Just open space and infinite directions and the quiet hum of a damaged ship limping toward somewhere.

Jarik leaned back in his chair. His hands, which had been shaking earlier, had finally steadied. His heartbeat had returned to something approaching normal. The adrenaline was fading, leaving behind exhaustion and the distant realization that he'd survived something he probably shouldn't have.

"Val, where's the nearest station?"

"Checking. Closest is Theta Station. Four days at current speed." Val paused. "Though I should mention— we're wanted there."

"Of course we are."

"There's a smaller outpost in Beta Quadrant. Six days. Less official presence. Questionable customs enforcement."

"Questionable how?"

"They once let a ship through that was ninety percent contraband and ten percent ship." Val's voice carried a note of admiration. "Flexible regulations."

"Set course for the outpost."

"Plotting. Also—" Val hesitated, "—incoming transmission."

Jarik's hands froze on the controls. "From?"

"Priority Alpha classification. Source: FRBL Central Command."

The peaceful moment evaporated. Jarik's heart rate spiked back up. "They found us already?"

"Unclear. The transmission is on a general broadcast frequency. Automated emergency response."

Brentley opened both eyes now, one ear slightly forward. "That'll be about the ship. Central Command knows the *Perpetual Compliance* imploded. They're scrambling to figure out what happened before Greeb's report arrives."

"Ignore it," Jarik said firmly.

"Message reads: 'All vessels are advised that an incident has occurred at coordinates—'" Val paused, "—the coordinates of where we just were. 'FRBL vessel lost. Investigation pending. Any information regarding Familiar-7734 should be reported immediately. Director Archimor has assumed oversight of—'"

"Cut it off," Jarik said.

The transmission ended mid-word. Silence filled the cabin.

Brentley's purr resumed. "See? They don't know if I'm alive or dead. They just know their shiny new ship turned into glitter. Once Greeb files his report, the case closes."

"And until then?"

"Until then, we stay quiet and let bureaucracy do what it does best." The cat's ears swiveled. "Move slowly."

"Though I'm curious about Director Archimor getting involved. He usually doesn't handle field operations. He's one of the Old Ones. Been with the Bureau since before it was even called the Bureau—back when it was just a loose agreement between agitated wizards who wanted their cats to stop disappearing." Brentley's eyes narrowed. "If he's personally requesting debrief, the Bureau is taking this very seriously."

"They're going to hunt us forever." Jarik slumped in his chair.

"Hunt me? Absolutely. They've been hunting me for three months. Another few months won't make a difference." His whiskers twitched. "Though I do wonder if Admiral Bubbles and Corvus made it somewhere safe. They had the mayonnaise with them. That's either very good or very bad."

"I'm not going to ask."

"Wise choice."

"That's not reassuring!"

"Wasn't meant to be." The cat's eyes gleamed. "But look at the bright side—your life just got infinitely more interesting."

"I don't want interesting! I want boring! I want safe!" Jarik's voice climbed. "I want to haul freight without talking cats and reality-warping hairballs and space bureaucrats!"

"Too late for that." Brentley yawned. "You're documented now. In their system. Your ship's signature is flagged. Even if you dropped me off tomorrow, they'd still want to interview you."

"Interview?"

"Extensively. With forms. So many forms. Might as well keep me around. At least I'm entertaining."

Jarik slumped forward, resting his forehead on the console. The cool metal felt good against his skin. Around him, his ship groaned. Behind him, small flames crackled. And beside him, a cat purred with absolute confidence.

"This is a nightmare," he muttered.

"This is adventure." Brentley's voice was closer now. The cat had moved, sitting right next to Jarik's elbow. "You were dying slowly in this ship. Boring routes. Bad coffee. No purpose beyond the next delivery."

"That was safe."

"That was sad." The cat's tail swished, brushing against Jarik's arm. "Now you have stories. Scars. Something to remember."

"I'm going to remember this as the day my life fell apart."

"Or the day it started. Perspective is everything."

Jarik lifted his head, looking at the cat. Really looking. At the orange fur that somehow survived vacuum. At the eyes that were far too intelligent. At the complete, absolute certainty in every movement.

"What are you?" he asked. "Really."

"A cat." Brentley's tail swished. "With opinions. And skills. And a flexible relationship with physics."

"That's not an answer."

"It's the only answer you'll get tonight." The cat stood, stretched, and padded toward the captain's chair. "I'm tired. Destroying ships is exhausting. All that running. The zero-G. The hairball."

"You were napping through most of it!"

"Exactly. Exhausting." Brentley hopped onto the chair, circling twice before settling down. "Wake me when we reach somewhere interesting. Or dangerous. Preferably both."

"What if I want to go somewhere safe?"

"Then you'll be very bored. And I'll complain loudly." The cat's eyes closed. "Your choice."

Jarik stared at him. At the cat who'd destroyed a government ship, talked his way out of arrest, and was now napping in his chair like he owned it.

"We're dropping you off at that outpost," he said.

"Mm-hmm."

"I mean it."

"Of course you do."

"Six days. Then you're someone else's problem."

"So determined. I respect that." Brentley's purr deepened. "Wrong, but determined."

"I'm not wrong!"

"We'll see." The cat's tail curled around his nose. "Six days is a long time. Lots can happen. Ships can malfunction. Courses can change. Minds can reconsider."

"None of that is happening."

"If you say so." Brentley's voice was already fading toward sleep. "Though you should know—I'm extremely persuasive when I want to be."

"You're extremely annoying when you want to be."

"Same thing."

Jarik wanted to argue. Wanted to list all the reasons this partnership—not partnership, situation—couldn't continue. The danger. The warrants. The inevitable Bureau pursuit. The hairballs.

But the cat was already asleep, purring softly, completely at peace.

And Jarik found he didn't have the energy to shout at a sleeping cat.

He turned back to the controls. Checked the course to the outpost. Six days. He could survive six days. Drop off the cat. File for ship repairs. Maybe change his name and move to a different sector.

Start over. Again.

The thought was exhausting.

Through the viewport, stars wheeled past. The ship groaned. The small flames in the galley finally went out, leaving just smoke and the lingering smell of burnt plastic.

In the captain's chair, Brentley purred.

And despite everything—the damage, the warrants, the absolute insanity of the past few hours—Jarik felt something shift in his chest. Not acceptance. Not quite. But something close.

The universe had thrown a cat at his windshield. The cat had destroyed a government ship. And now Jarik was wanted in seven sectors—*seven, not nine, and he wasn't going to think about why that number had changed*—flying a damaged ship toward a questionable outpost, with a passenger who filed imaginary paperwork and spoke in riddles.

Objectively, the worst day of his life.

And yet.

"I should've left you on the windshield." But there was no heat in it.

Brentley's purr deepened, satisfied and knowing and entirely too smug.

"But you didn't."

Jarik looked at his ship—hull at sixty-eight percent, engines running on spite—then at the cat curled in his chair, purring like this was exactly where he was meant to be.

This is insane, he thought. *I'm terrified. And somehow more alive than I've been in years.*

"No," he said quietly. "I didn't."

And despite himself, despite everything, Jarik smiled. Actually smiled. Not the brief flicker from before, but something real.

Somewhere, probably, the Bureau was filing forms. That was a problem for tomorrow. He set their course—six days to the outpost, six days to figure out what came next—and steered them forward.

Brentley watched the stars drift past, one eye opening slightly. "I should tell you something."

"I don't want to hear it."

"The reason I was really in that sector—" The cat's tail twitched. "I was looking for someone."

Despite himself, Jarik asked: "Who?"

"My practitioner." Brentley's purr went quiet. "The one I actually chose."

Jarik didn't answer right away. He couldn't. The words went somewhere quiet.

The one I actually chose.

The phrasing stopped him—*actually chose* doing all the heavy lifting, implying the existence of one he hadn't. Of bonds he carried because they had been arranged or assumed or taken. Brentley didn't elaborate. He didn't have to. The phrase had said exactly as much as he wanted it to and nothing more.

It was also the first thing Brentley had said all day that

didn't sound like a performance. No flourish. No qualifier. No careful pivot toward absurdism. Just a statement, quiet and exact, from a cat who specialized in being neither.

"Why tell me?" Jarik asked.

Brentley was still watching the stars. "Because you didn't ask. And the ones who don't ask are the only ones worth telling."

The purr did not return. Not for a long time. Long enough that Jarik wondered if Brentley regretted the saying of it, or if the silence was itself the saying—the kind of quiet that meant *I have given you something I cannot take back.*

He didn't ask again. He let the cat keep his question.

But the course he'd already set—toward the rimward outpost—felt different now. Six days through the dark with a cat who specialized in lying and had just told him something true. Somewhere out there, in that direction or near it, was someone Brentley had chosen. Someone real enough to drive a cat into Bureau territory. Someone worth a hairball-sized hole in a government vessel.

Someone Jarik now, against every instinct that had kept him alive in cargo work for six years, was steering toward.

And the stars wheeled on, indifferent and beautiful and full of stories waiting to be told.

INCIDENT REPORT FORM 9-B (REVISED)

CLASSIFICATION: OMEGA

Report ID: IR-7734-26-FINAL

Filing Officer: Enforcement Director Greeb (Badge #4427)

Date Filed: 3rd Cycle, 14th Rotation, Standard Year 2852

Incident Type: ☐ Routine Recapture ☐ Escape ☑ Catastrophic Loss

Vessel Lost: FRBL *Perpetual Compliance* (Registry FRBL-0447-E)

SUMMARY OF INCIDENT

On the date referenced above, Enforcement Team 7734-R boarded civilian cargo vessel *Marginal Profit* (Registry CV-8842) in pursuit of escaped familiar designated 7734. Intelligence suggested Subject may be aboard said vessel in violation of

Regulation 15-D (Harboring of Unregistered Familiars).

Initial containment protocols proceeded according to standard procedure until the civilian vessel experienced cascading system failures, including but not limited to: coffee machine explosion, gravity stabilization collapse, and backup power malfunction. These failures appear to have been pre-existing conditions unrelated to Bureau operations.

During resultant zero-gravity conditions, a Class-7 Reality Residue (hereafter: "the hairball") of unknown origin manifested in the civilian vessel. Despite immediate containment attempts by trained personnel, said hairball demonstrated autonomous locomotion and entered FRBL *Perpetual Compliance* via docking tube, where it then reached the vessel's hyperdrive core.

The *Perpetual Compliance* experienced immediate dimensional collapse and total structural failure. The implosion occurred at 0855 hours.

All Bureau personnel were successfully evacuated prior to implosion. No civilian casualties occurred. Subject 7734's status

following the reality breach incident
remains indeterminate.

Casualties: 0 (zero)
Vessel Status: Total loss
Subject Status: INDETERMINATE (see
Section 7)

DETAILED SEQUENCE OF EVENTS

0847 Hours: Enforcement Team 7734-R
successfully boarded *Marginal Profit*.
Subject 7734 located. Containment collar
prepared.

0849 Hours: Civilian vessel's coffee
machine exploded.

0850 Hours: Gravity stabilizers failed. All
personnel entered zero-G conditions.

0851 Hours: Enforcement Officer Talon and
Enforcement Officer Clover experienced
spatial disorientation. Minor collision
occurred. No injuries sustained.

0852 Hours: Subject 7734 produced hairball.
Scanners immediately classified residue as
Class-7 Reality Hazard.

0853 Hours: Hairball demonstrated autonomous locomotion. Entered FRBL *Perpetual Compliance* via docking tube despite containment attempts.

0854 Hours: Hairball reached hyperdrive core.

0855 Hours: *Perpetual Compliance* imploded.

0856 Hours: This officer activated emergency beacon and requested immediate extraction.

WITNESS STATEMENT: ENFORCEMENT OFFICER TALON

We boarded the *Marginal Profit* in pursuit of Subject 7734. Initial scan results were inconclusive due to interference from the vessel's malfunctioning systems.

During the gravity failure, a glowing hairball manifested. Origin unclear. The hairball moved with apparent purpose toward our vessel. I attempted interception but was unable to maintain flight trajectory in zero-gravity conditions due to involuntary wing extension. I collided with Officer Clover. This was not Officer Clover's fault.

When the *Perpetual Compliance* imploded, I was unable to maintain visual contact with the civilian vessel's interior. Post-incident scans revealed no definitive traces of Subject 7734.

I recommend extreme caution should any future reports of Subject 7734 surface. Though I sincerely hope they will not.

WITNESS STATEMENT: ENFORCEMENT OFFICER CLOVER

Everything was very confusing and I would like to go home now.

Something glowed. It rolled past me. I tried to catch it but my holster was oriented wrong and I accidentally discharged my stunner into the wall panel which I am very sorry about.

The hairball went into our ship and then the ship wasn't there anymore and there were sparkles everywhere.

I don't know what happened to the cat. The scanners didn't work right.

Director Greeb said we're getting reassigned to Filing Division. I like filing. Filing doesn't explode.

Thank you for your consideration.

SECTION 7: SUBJECT STATUS AND QUANTUM SIGNATURE ANALYSIS

Post-incident scans of the debris field revealed no biological traces matching Subject 7734's profile. However, quantum signature readings were inconclusive.

Standard biology scan: **NEGATIVE**
DNA trace analysis: **NEGATIVE**
Magical signature detection: **INDETERMINATE**
Probability assessment: **ERROR - CONFLICTING DATA**
Quantum state observation: **SUBJECT IS/IS NOT PRESENT (UNRESOLVED)**

Per Regulation 44-F (Classification of

Uncertain Outcomes), subjects whose quantum signatures cannot be definitively resolved following Class-7 Reality Events may be classified as **PRESUMED NEUTRALIZED.**

SECTION 8: PROPERTY DAMAGE ASSESSMENT

Bureau Property Lost:

- FRBL *Perpetual Compliance* (Enforcement Vessel, Mark VII)
- Containment collar (enchanted, Grade-A)
- Seventeen clipboards (twelve standard, five enchanted)
- One dragonhide evidence satchel
- Forty-seven regulation manuals (hardcopy)
- Six hundred and thirty-two pre-filled forms (various)

Estimated Total Cost: 437,000 credits

SECTION 9: RECOMMENDATIONS

I. Subject 7734 should be classified

as **PRESUMED NEUTRALIZED** effective immediately.

2. Case file 7734 should be moved to **CLOSED/ARCHIVED** status.

3. No further pursuit of Subject 7734 is recommended at this time due to:
   - Quantum indeterminacy
   - Resource allocation concerns
   - Extreme hazard classification
   - This officer's mental health

4. Civilian vessel operator Jarik Venn should be released with warning. Subject was victim of circumstance. (See attached Form 2847-B: Statement of Non-Involvement)

5. All personnel involved in incident should receive:
   - Mandatory counseling (Form 88-C filed)
   - Reassignment to low-risk duties
   - Hazard pay adjustment for reality exposure
   - This officer would like a vacation

6. Coffee machines should be added to pre-boarding safety checklist.

SECTION 10: FILING OFFICER'S PERSONAL NOTES

I have pursued Subject 7734 for three months. I have filled out 2,473 forms. I have lost a ship. My clipboard broke.

The quantum readings say he might be gone. The readings also say he might not be. The readings mostly say the readings don't know.

I am choosing to believe he is gone.

I am also choosing to believe he is very, very far away from my jurisdiction.

If Subject 7734 is somehow still alive and operating in other sectors, I respectfully recommend they become someone else's problem. Preferably someone in a different galaxy.

This case is closed.

DO NOT REOPEN.

Authorized Signature: *Enforcement Director Greeb*
Date: 3rd Cycle, 14th Rotation, Standard Year 2852
Badge Number: 4427

Approved By: *Director Archimor*

Approval Statement: The cat who was not a cat walks roads unseeable to eyes that seek what cannot be held. The paperwork reflects the moon's shadow at noon. File in triplicate.

Translation (per Protocol 19-G): Approved. Close the case.

CASE STATUS: CLOSED

SUBJECT 7734 STATUS: PRESUMED NEUTRALIZED

RECOMMENDATION: DO NOT PURSUE FURTHER

CHARACTER LIST

The Marginal Profit (and Passengers)

Brentley: An orange tabby cat of questionable origin and even more questionable honesty. Formerly designated Familiar-7734 by the Bureau. Currently: wanted in nine sectors, destroyer of government property, and self-proclaimed freelance miracle. His lies occasionally rewrite reality, his hairballs destroy starships, and his ego remains magnificently intact. On his ninth and final life, which he's spending exactly how he pleases—causing chaos, avoiding capture, and taking credit for accidents.

Jarik Venn: Cargo hauler. Former believer in boring, safe routes. Current accessory to familiar harboring and unintentional participant in bureaucratic disasters. Pilots the *Marginal Profit,* a ship held together by optimism, spite, and increasingly poor decisions. Has gone from "I should've left you on the windshield" to reluctant partnership in approximately three hours. Still processing this.

Val: Ship AI of the *Marginal Profit*. Remarkably patient given the circumstances. Provides status reports with increasing resignation. Notable for translating bureaucratic nonsense, surviving multiple explosions, and maintaining basic sarcasm subroutines through catastrophic system failures. The door still thinks it's closed.

Familiar Reclamation Bureau of Licensing

Enforcement Director Greeb: Pembroke Welsh Corgi. Bureau field agent promoted specifically to recapture Brentley after the "tragic paperwork accident." Carries a glowing clipboard, quotes regulations by number, and has filled out 2,473 forms because of one cat. Professional, exhausted, and surprisingly reasonable about the whole ship-implosion situation. Three demotions and counting.

Enforcement Officer Talon: Owl. Professional, observant, prone to involuntary wing extension during zero-gravity incidents. Member of Enforcement Team 7734-R. Recommends Subject 7734 never be pursued again. Currently reassigned to Filing Division, where the biggest hazard is paper cuts.

Enforcement Officer Clover: Rabbit. Earnest, apologetic, experiencing ongoing confusion about recent events. Member of Enforcement Team 7734-R. Would prefer not to work on any more cases involving cats, hairballs, reality hazards, or coffee machines. Currently reassigned to Filing Division. Likes filing. Filing doesn't explode.

Director Archimor: Celestial owl. Speaks entirely in riddles that mean absolutely nothing. Head of Bureau operations. Requested immediate debrief following the *Perpetual Compliance* incident. Known for making situations more confusing, not less.

The Perpetual Compliance Crew: Approximately forty-seven additional Bureau personnel. Maintenance staff, filing clerks, junior analysts, and one very stressed janitorial familiar (species: raccoon). All successfully evacuated before implosion. None willing to discuss the incident. Several have requested immediate transfer to landlocked facilities.

Escaped, Missing, or Otherwise Unaccounted For...

Admiral Bubbles: Goldfish. Wears a mechanical combat suit with manipulator arms and forward-mounted lasers. Escaped the Bureau facility alongside Brentley through unclear means involving catnip and questionable decisions. Current location: unknown. Relationship status with haunted mayonnaise: also unknown.

Corvus: Raven. Prophet of doom and strategic betrayer/ally (it's complicated). Last seen flying away from the Bureau escape while prophesying about paperwork multiplication and silent audits. Her loyalties remain as uncertain as her predictions.

The Haunted Mayonnaise: Jar. Glows ominously. Classification: Class-7 Reality Hazard. Caused the scanner to explode during processing. Removed from containment by Admiral Bubbles. Current status: undefined. Preferred not to elaborate.

Gerald: Sentient paperclip. Former Bureau office supply. Bound by enchantment three hundred years ago and forced into filing duties ever since. Deeply dissatisfied with his career trajectory. Assisted in Subject 7734's escape after being promised freedom. Current status: unknown. Last seen questioning his entire existence while picking locks. Represents the hopes and dreams of office supplies everywhere.

The Coffee Machine: Antagonist. Destroyer of ships. Catalyst of chaos. Exploded at the worst possible moment and compromised the gravity stabilizers. Responsible for approximately 40% of the plot. Now a memory. Still no apology.

THE OVERLORDS
HAVE OPINIONS

Enjoyed this book?

Reviews help other readers find these stories! If you have a moment, leaving a review on Amazon, Goodreads, or your retailer of choice means the world to indie authors like me.

Want a free short story?

Sign up for my newsletter and get 2 short stories from my other series. **kysasteele.com/newsletter**

Buy direct (the overlords thank you)

Signed paperbacks and DRM-free ebooks are available straight from me at **kysasteele.com**. More of each sale skips the middlemen and goes to the author—which means, realistically, to the cats. They have expensive tastes.

WANT MORE CATS AND CHAOS?

Join my Patreon for weekly chapter drops, exclusive stories, world-building lore, and behind-the-scenes chaos at

patreon.com/kysasteele

ABOUT THE AUTHOR

Kysa Steele is an IT professional by day, and by night an author, TTRPG GM, cat servant, and wife (though the order depends on which cat is asking). She grew up devouring books and plotting to write her own. While newly minted as an indie author, she's been telling elaborate, occasionally cursed stories at the TTRPG table for years.

Her cat-centric fiction spans dark fantasy, detective noir, portal adventures, and apocalyptic comedy. The Infurnal Catastrophe series features a cursed demon princess and infernal magic, while the Orange Protocol follows a hard-boiled detective trapped in a cat's body and scattered across a psychic network of orange tabbies. Her Unfamiliar Territory series stars Mischief, a portal-hopping cat whose curiosity threatens entire dimensions. She spends her time building worlds and trying to unravel her cats' many conspiracies.

She lives in Texas with her husband and a cadre of furry overlords. Nori and Mochi are the latest recruits, while Nox, nicknamed the Demon Princess, claimed dominion during the writing of Curse Meow Not. Jake Speed and his sister Ripley occupy the middle ranks, and the eldest, Cid, remains her watchful shadow and self-appointed bodyguard.

ALSO BY KYSA STEELE

The Infurnal Catastrophe

DARK FANTASY WITH CLAWS

1. Curse Meow Not
2. Forget Meow Not
3. Leave Meow Not (2027)

Nine Lives, Infinite Lies

ABSURDIST SPACE COMEDY

1. Nine Lives, Zero Paperwork
2. Nine Lives, One Witness (Aug 8, 2026)

Orange Protocol

SURREAL CAT NOIR

1. Containment Not Recommended
2. Signal Integrity Compromised (2027)

Unfamiliar Territory

PORTAL FANTASY, MAXIMUM SNARK

1. Cat Out of Luck

Tales of Festive Misrule

A Krampus holiday cozy duology

1. The Twelve Days of Catmas
2. The Kitten Clause (*Dec 5 2026*)

The Cats of Opal Manor

Cozy chapter books for young readers

1. The Long Way Home (*Sep 12 2026*)

Standalones

Handle with Care

Quiet and emotional (bring tissues)

The Cat That Time Built (*Oct 31 2026*)

A grief-soaked clockwork fable

The Cat Who Ate the End of the World

Apocalyptic comedy

The Feline Guide to Surviving Your Human Workplace

Deadpan workplace satire